Diamantha Pearl

Only Intimacy

The Meeting

2024 Goozlyzo

First Edition: MARCH 6, 2024
Copyright: Diamantha Pearl
Copyright: Goozlyzo
ISBN: 9789083425207

This book is dedicated to you...

You, who are horny!

You, who don't dare yet!

You, who can't get enough,

You, who still need help,

You, who are still dry,

You, who want a change.

Yes, I'm here for you...

Story 1

After a long working year, it is finally time for a holiday. I often go to nude beaches abroad. It's nice and anonymous. Strange country, strange location, strange people. Delicious.

I lie comfortably on my bath towel. It is secluded and quiet here on the beach.
I take off my pants and my T-shirt. Of course, my boxers can't be missed either. Who lies down on a naked beach with their clothes on?
There is a lady next to me, about 100 meters away. She has two nicely shaped buttocks and muscular legs. I suspect she is in her late 30s. She has dark hair and beautiful, tanned skin.
I had the impression for a moment that we had eye contact.
What a tight round ass she has, I think to myself.
What am I doing? I thought.
I'm on a run to the sea.
I'll take a dip right away.
It is so tasty. The sea is neither too cold nor too warm. Exactly right.
I feel a drop. I looked up. There are no clouds, but suddenly, it starts to rain heavily. I ran out of the water. I grab my things and run behind a shelter.
The tanned lady lying next to me also runs to the shelter.
I don't understand why everyone is running away. Only me and her were left behind.
Well, it's not a shelter. It's more of a cabin. A clap of thunder startles us both.
There we are. Both are naked with wet clothes.

"There we are," she says, smiling.
"Yes, that happened so quickly. It might have something to do

with global warming," I said.

"You think?" she says, looking deep into my eyes.

I feel it warming up down there with me.

The tension is palpable.

She starts laughing. "I think it's getting wet in here, too."

Before I could answer, she put her hand on my penis. She feels the glans with one finger. A bit of pre-cum was already coming out.

"It is indeed wet; has it rained there too?" she says.

"Let's see if there's a thunderstorm in your area too," I say. It's also nice and wet.

"I want to explore you deeper; is that allowed?" I whisper in her ear.

"Yessss," she said.

I caress the inside of her thighs with the top of my hand.

She makes a teasing circle on my glans with her index finger. I rub two fingers between her labia. I feel that they are wet too. Furthermore, I alternate squeezing and massaging. I continue with my hand.

Aha, I found her clitoris.

That smell of sea and horniness. That's a perfect combination.

I get down on my knees in front of her. I run my tongue from top to bottom and from bottom to top over her pussy. I do the same movement faster and faster.

I place my hand near her belly button, so I can feel her body's reaction.

She starts to shake. I go deeper, faster, and harder with my tongue.

Wow, what does just my tongue do to someone? I thought.

With my hand, I open her labia so that I can suck her clitoris.

"AAAAA," she says shakily. Or did she moan? I have no idea; I just have my full attention on her clitoris.

"Fuck me, now," she says, moaning.

I get up. She turns around.

I push my penis into her from behind. The famous Doggystyle.

Oh, that's hot and wet. Blessed!

I grab her breasts with my hand as I thrust. Harder and harder.

As I thrust harder, the thunder also raged. I hear thunderbolts.

Somehow, it makes me wilder and wilder. The harder the
lightning blows, the harder I punch.

"I'm coming; I'm coming," she says.

Moaning, with a few deep and hard thrusts, I come inside her.

She screams out, "AAAAA".

I take my penis out of her vagina. All the cum is dripping off.

It's still raining.

"Shall we go another round?" I said, panting.

She starts laughing.

I think we're going to stay here for a while; there's no sign that it
will stop anytime soon," she says.

**DIAMANTHA: "As I hear here, you had a nice experience.
What's the problem? I ask Richard.**

Richard: "I wasn't done with my story."

Richard continues...

After that day, I went to that nude beach again.

I was sunbathing in my nude, of course.

Suddenly, a brunette lady stands in front of me.

"Hey," she says.

She spontaneously comes and sits next to me.

I'm so surprised that someone would just come up to me.

She held out her hand. "I'm Nady," she says.

I've heard good things about you.

"What have you heard?" I asked her, surprisingly.

A friend of mine told me that she had fucked a tourist here.
She had described you, and I recognized you by your tattoo on
your right side.
"I have a heart tattoo with an R in it," I said.
She stands up suddenly.
"Let's go for a walk."
I get up and follow her.
We walk into the dunes. There's no one there.
She stands still.
"Open your mouth," she says.
I open my mouth. She puts her fingers in my mouth and slowly
lowers her other hand. Her hands reach my balls. She squeezes it
gently.
I keep looking ahead. Let's see if no one comes and catches us.
She takes her hand out of my mouth and starts massaging my
penis. While her other hand massages my balls. I, in turn, visit
her body. I can feel with my hand how soft her legs are.
She presses her hips against my hips. I place one hand on her ass
and the other hand on her pussy. She opens her legs wider, so I
can reach them more easily. My hand reaches her full labia. I
massage them gently.
"Fuck me like you fucked my girlfriend," she whispers in my ear.
At that moment, I inserted three fingers. It scares her.
My finger massages her vagina. It feels slippery, horny, and
warm. She also starts pulling my penis harder.
I can't hold on anymore.
I turn her around, and she bends down. I quickly put my penis in
her vagina. I start thrusting hard.
She starts to scream with pleasure.
"Scream quieter," I told her.
"We're about to get caught."
Her screaming, combined with the thought that we could be

caught at any time, turns me on. And that makes me thrust harder.
"I'm coming," I said.
She quickly takes a step forward.
"Wait," she says.
She turns around. She kneels in front of me and puts my penis in her mouth.
I feel my orgasm coming, and I start breathing more heavily.
I cum in her mouth. She swallowed every drop.

She smiles and stands up.
Not only that, but she looks deep into my eyes and runs away.

Diamantha: "What is your problem? Why are you here?" I asked Richard.

Richard: "Well, I can't forget her face. That intense look."
Diamantha looks at her alarm clock. The alarm goes off.
Diamantha: "Your time is up." We will continue at the next appointment."

Diamantha to you: "Richard's story continues in Part 2. Will I see you then?"

Story 2

We were a nice group of friends. Me, John, Devany, and Frank.
But since that night, everything has changed.

It is Saturday, May 10th. I'm celebrating my 28th birthday in a
holiday home that I rented.
I invited my friends and family. The house was full. After dancing
and eating a lot, the party ended at 3 am.
The four of us were left behind: John, Devany, Frank, and I.
I was cleaning up in the kitchen.
John hugged me from behind.
"Do you have any more wishes, Mrs. Raida?" he asked me.
"Yes, a pleasant dance with you," I replied defiantly.
I can smell from his breath that John has drunk quite a lot.
He's not going to drive a car anymore, I thought.
I turn around, and he kisses me on the mouth.
"Congratulations, darling," he said.
Denavy and Frank are talking at a table in the living room.
John and I saw Frank massaging Devany's buttocks.
John looks at me. He puts his hand on my buttock.
"You have a much nicer butt than Devany," he whispers in my
ear.
I start laughing, and he squeezes my buttocks.
It scares me.
That's exciting, I thought to myself.
In the meantime, we look at Devany and Frank. We do exactly
what they do. Frank squeezes Devany's buttocks. He puts his
hands in the back of the dress and feels her warm buttocks.
John puts his hands in my pants to reach my buttocks.
"What soft buttocks do you have!" he said.

Frank sat down on a chair. Devany takes off her dress and sits on his lap, teasingly. She was teasingly sliding her ass on his penis.

John stands behind me and teasingly rubs his penis against my ass.

"Ah, what are you doing to me?" says Frank, panting.

"I haven't even started yet," Devany told Frank.

John pinches my hard nipples.

"Are you enjoying the view?" he asked me, looking at Devany and Frank.

John slowly started to open the button on my pants. And he slowly slides his hand into my underwear. He feels my wet labia.

I hear Devany and Frank groaning.

As he massaged my labia with his fingers, he gave me a hickey on my neck.

"Harder," I said.

"What should I do harder?" he asked me.

"Suck me harder, please," I said, biting my lips.

Frank takes off Devany's bra and sucks her nipples.

"Mmm...," Devany moans.

I think it's hot to see Devany enjoying herself.

I turn around and kiss John fiercely as I slide my hand into his pants.

I can't reach it very well, so I open his pants.

And start playing with his penis.

"I never knew you had such a big penis," I said.

He puts his hand in my underwear.

"You're nice and wet; are you horny for my cock?" he asked.

He puts his hand deeper into my vagina. He takes his hand out of my vagina and puts it in my mouth.

"Taste your horniness," he said.

With my moist mouth, I bend over his penis and put it in my mouth.

I put it all in my mouth.
What a delicious sausage this is, I thought.
I take the penis out of my mouth to see what Devany and Frank
are doing.
Frank moaned, and I saw cum coming out of Devany's mouth.
Devany gets up and walks towards me and John.
She bends down next to me.
"Shall we do it together?" she asked me.
"Yes, horny," I said.
We divided the penis fairly.
She sucks on the left side, and I suck on the right side.
After a while, John started squirting. He sprayed both our faces.
Devany continues to undress me. And I continue to undress her.
We continued naked on the couch in the living room. The boys
came, but we didn't. So it's our turn now. John and Frank sat
down in front of us to watch our show.
I went with my leg wide open, and Devany bent over on her knee
with her ass in front of John and Frank.
Devany and I started French kissing. We played with each other's
breasts. I lay on my back, and she lay on me in the famous 69
position. We started eating each other's pussy.
I enjoyed every tongue movement that Devany made.
We stopped eating out and looked at Frank and John. We saw
that they were excited. Both had hard penises.
Our eye contact said it all. They stood up.
Devany and I sat on the chair with our asses up.
Frank put his penis in me. And John put his penis in Devany.
All four of us started to moan with pleasure.
The harder they thrust, the louder we moaned.
All four of us came at the same time.

**Diamantha: "And the problem now is that the friendship is no
longer the same?" I asked Raida.**

Diamantha to readers: "Raida's story continues in Part 2. Will I see you then?"

Story 3

I immediately stepped on the brake pedal when I saw the red light. The car came to a stop just in time.
"Shit!"
It always happens when it is inconvenient. "Why now, car trouble?"
I drive the car along the road. I stop the car and turn it off. Furthermore, I wait 5 minutes and turn the car back on. There is no red light on anymore. I decided to continue driving the car and visit the garage the next day. Or I can have my neighbor look at it.

I know this road very well; I drive here every day. Was it the weather that kept me distracted, or something else? I can't remember anymore. It was so hot in the car. I had no air conditioning because it had given up long ago.
A golden Ferrari passes me.
"What is he even thinking? I have priority!"
I accelerated hard to overtake him. I approached him. I make a hand gesture, even though I know he certainly can't see. He looked at me in his rearview mirror and raised his middle finger. I raised my middle finger as well.
I took a deep breath. It was about 37 degrees. I can feel the sweat rolling down my forehead. I drove on, and I didn't see him anymore.
Suddenly, I felt someone was watching me. I looked over and was shocked. It was that Ferrari from over there. He rolled down his window. "Sorry, but my middle finger is bigger than yours," he said kindly.
I think he's in his early forties. He had brown hair and stubble. And very beautiful blue eyes.

Nice handsome man, expensive car, and a friendly jerk, I
thought. What kind of job would he have? Maybe something in
marketing or sales. Or maybe he has his own company. He is an
interesting man.
"How did you get your driver's license? Don't you know any
traffic rules?" I asked.
"Shall I buy you a nice coffee ?" he asked.
I frowned. "Are you serious?" I asked.
"Yes, I mean it. Follow me," he said.
I drove after him.
Of course, with my car, it's quite difficult to keep up. He had
arrived at Café Le Marind before me.
It is a well-known café. I stepped inside. A bartender came up to
me. "Mr. Tentad is waiting for you; follow me," he said.
We walk to an office. Everything was made of oak. I looked
around further.
Then he came in and shook my hand. "I'm Tony Tentad, owner of
this café. And several other companies," he said.
I guessed right, I thought.
"I thought we were going for coffee, so why am I here? We can
sit in the café, right?"
"I want to offer you my coffee; this is a unique and special
coffee," he said.
"You're kidding, right?" I said.
What a confident, arrogant bastard, I thought.
He keeps looking straight at me. I also keep looking straight back
at him.
He continued, "We're going upstairs to my apartment. In my
bedroom, I have a queen-size bed. I ordered you to take off your
clothes. And choose a piece of lingerie from my collection. Then
you lie on my comfy bed. I do take off my clothes and lie next to
you. I lie on your side so that I can caress your body with my

hands. My fingers follow the contour of your bra, and your nipples become hard. Hard with desire, hard with horniness. You would like me to touch your nipples, but I don't. I let my fingers slide over your stomach. I go slowly towards your pants. You open your legs for me. I feel you already long for me. I'll let you stand with your legs open. I stand up and look at you. I see you have no control over your body. I'm going to sit with my legs spread over you. I'll take off your bra and pants. You take a deep breath. I don't know if it's from desire or shyness. I run my tongue along your hard nipples and then along your navel. You moan. You say, " Lick me, please. I run my tongue along your clitoral area. You scream with pleasure and cum. I turn you over. You lie on your stomach on the bed. I lie on top of you and come with my penis inside you. You're clinging to the sheets. You buried your head into the pillow. You scream in pleasure. Furthermore, you cum again. You ask me not to stop. I keep thrusting. You're moaning again."

"What did you do?" I asked Denna.

I can hardly believe what he was saying. I don't understand why men like him think that we women immediately open our legs because they are successful.

"I think it's better than coffee. Don't you think?" he said.

I must honestly admit that his proposal made me horny.
I looked straight at him and said, "No, thanks."
With a lot of self-control and self-confidence, I said, "I don't get turned on by such arrogant men as you."
I walked out of the café, laughing. He was left in amazement.

"It's good that you can control yourself well," I said to Denna.

"Yes, I am proud of my reaction," said Denna.

"Then, why are you here?", I asked.

When I got home, I stopped by my neighbor. He is a car mechanic.

I ring the bell. He opens the door.

"Hey, Denna. How are you? Come in," he said.

"Do you want something to drink?"

"What do you have?" I asked.

"Coffee, tea, soft drinks? I think Sprite would be nice in this weather."

"Yes, that's OK."

I sat down on the couch. He puts the drinks on the side table and sits next to me.

"I thought of you because I saw a red light on the dashboard. I don't know anything about cars. For my safety, I want you to take a look at it," I said.

"I can certainly help you. Give me your number, and I will let you know when I will pick up the keys."

We exchanged phone numbers.

I took a quick look at his pants. I still have Tony's story in my mind. I drank the Sprite very quickly and stood up.

"I'm going again. I had a busy day today. Let me know when you have time."

The next morning, I was still in bed. Who's going to get up early on Saturday morning?

I love sleeping naked. Especially with this warm weather. I decided to send Henry a message.

"Hey neighbor, good morning. Do you know when you have time
to look at my car?"
I heard the doorbell ring. I put on my bathrobe and walked to
the door.
I open the door. Yep, it's the neighbor.
"Hey, I just texted you," I said to Henry.
"I hadn't read it yet. I thought I now had some time to take a
look at your car. Do you have the keys for me?"
"Yes, I'll get them for you."
I walk to the kitchen table, grab the keys, walk back to the front
door, and hand him the keys.
"Would you like a cup of coffee?"
"Yes, please!"
"Come on in."
He comes in and takes a seat at the dining table.
I grab two cups from the cupboard and turn on the coffee
machine.
I take the cups with me, put them on the table, and sit directly
opposite him. He takes a sugar cube from a box on the table. He
accidentally dropped it. He slides down to grab the sugar cube
from the ground. At that moment, I accidentally opened my legs
so he could see that I was not wearing any pants. He looked at
my bald pussy. He came up again.
"I wanted to go to the beach today. But that's not possible if I
don't have a car. So it's going to be a nice series day today."
"Shall we look at your car? Maybe it's nothing serious. Then you
can still go to the beach today."
We drank the coffee and then walked to my car. He sits in the
driver's seat, and I sit in the other seat. He started reading the
car with a special device.
"Can that device read everything?" I asked Henry.
"Yes, in principle, yes, but of course I cannot guarantee that."

Due to my curiosity, I didn't notice that my bathrobe had
opened. And that he was looking at my chest.
I close my bathrobe again.
"I'm still working on the car."
"Then I'll continue doing things around the house."
"I'll come give you the key when I'm done."
I got out of the car and walked inside.

I was sitting on the couch watching television. What was I
watching? I have no idea. My thoughts were still with Tony, that
arrogant jerk from yesterday. I notice that I'm still horny.
A moment later, I heard the doorbell. I get up and walk to the
door. I open the door, and at that moment, I drop the bathrobe
on the floor. In fright, he dropped the car keys on the floor.
"Did you like what you saw in the kitchen and the car?" I
whispered in his ear.
He answered this question with a French kiss.
While we are kissing each other passionately, I feel his hands on
my breasts.
"Wait, close the door."
He closed the front door while he kissed me. He gently massages
my nipples with his hand.
We stopped kissing. I take off his t-shirt and feel his chest.
"Mmm, you go to the gym often."
Without me being able to continue talking, he stuck his tongue
in my mouth.
I slowly undress him further. We stand naked in front of each
other. He directs me to the couch in the living room. He pushes
me onto the couch. Furthermore, he lay on top of me and
started licking my neck. I moaned with pleasure.
"I hear you moaning. Are you up for it?" he asked.
Without me having time to answer, he bites me on my earlobe.

He kissed his way down to my navel. He came up and bit my neck. He makes circles with his tongue. Kissing, he runs his tongue back down my neck. He stops at my nipple. I moan again. He bites on one nipple while he massages the other nipple with one hand. I playfully pinch his nipple while he licks the other nipple. After a while, he takes turns.

Kissing, he goes down until he reaches my pussy.

"Mmm... You have a nice, sweet pussy. Mmm... Hot," he says.

He kisses me on my labia. He kisses and licks my groin. He moves further and further down with his mouth towards my knees.

He suddenly comes back to my pussy. I breathe deeply. I feel his warm breath on my clitoris. He goes back to kissing my knee. He comes back up to my pussy. He blows on it. I felt myself gasping for breath. I groan and put my hands on his head. He is going to play his tongue with my clitoris.

Wow, that's so hot.

In the meantime, he rubs my pussy with three fingers and gently presses all three fingers into my wet vagina. He fingers me back and forth, while still stimulating my clitoris with his tongue. He sucks on my clitoris.

I moaned with pleasure.

He slides two fingers into my vagina while pressing one finger against my ass.

I couldn't hold on anymore. I squirted in his mouth. I cum, but that wasn't a reason for him to stop eating cunnilingus.

"Stand up straight," he said.

I stood up straight. His cock had become hard from the horniness. I grab his penis and put it in my mouth. I started sucking as deep as I could.

Mmm... What a big and thick penis he has, I thought.

He puts his hands on my head and moves to the rhythm with which I blow. I let his penis slide over my tongue while sucking.

I stopped giving blowjobs. I start licking around his glans.
Furthermore, I open my mouth wide and stick my tongue out. He
hits my tongue with his penis. Then I put his penis deep in my
mouth again.
I think blowjobs are one of the most fun things there is to do.
This way, I feel that I have control over the man.
He groans.
You're doing very well, Denna, I thought.
In the meantime, I started playing with his balls with my hand.
"I'm almost here," he said.
I started blowing harder.
"Oh, Denna, oh," he said, groaning.
He filled my throat and mouth.
"Oh, you can do miracles with your mouth," he said, exhausted.
We both sat down on the couch. I put my hand on the penis
again.
Yeah, "I'm not done yet."
I start to play gently with his penis again.
"Lie on your back," I told him.
I sat on him.
"There, you're still wet," he said.
I start riding his penis while rubbing my clitoris.
"I, I, I..."
I quickly stand up and spray over his stomach.
I sit on the couch. He gets up and starts jerking off.
"Where do you want it?" he asked.
"Here," I said, pointing to my breasts.
After five minutes, he squirted all over my breasts.
"We don't have much time left," I say to Denna.
I'm going to finish my story soon.

After a few days, I had to pick up my car from the garage. I came
in, and no one was there. I walked to the back, where there was

a small office. The door was open.

"Hi, I'm Denna. I'm coming to pick up my car," I said.

It was a man in his late 40s with light brown eyes, clean-shaven and bald. His body was covered in tattoos.

"Ma'am, your car is not ready yet," he said.

His cool look made me so horny.

"I didn't cum either," blurted out of my mouth.

He suddenly looked at me with a beaming smile. He came to stand in front of me. He grabs my face with both of his dirty hands full of oil. He closed the door and started kissing me heavily.

"Is this what you wanted, right?" he said.

Kissing one of Henry's colleagues? No, that's not possible, I thought.

Our tongues play a fun game of horniness and desire for more. He lifted my dress. I took off his T-shirt. He not only has a tattoo on his arm but on his entire chest. It should form an anaconda. I pinch both his nipples with my fingers. He groans. I open his zipper.. I can feel that he already has a hard-on.

"Shall I help you?" he asked as he opened the button of his pants and lowered them slightly. A thick penis pops out. He's not as big as Henry.

I grab his balls with my hands. I massage them firmly until he starts to moan. I bent down and put my lips on his glans. My tongue makes circles around the head of his cock. I press my lips against his skin.

"What a horny woman you are," he said. He grabs me under my armpits and lifts me. He lays me on my back on the desk.

I slide my head to the edge of the desk and let it hang over it. He slides his penis deep into my throat. He starts moving back and forth with his penis in my mouth. Back and forth. Back and forth. And ever deeper. I feel my pussy getting wet. He takes his penis

out of my mouth. He takes my pants down. He licks my clitoral
area, he licks my labia, and he licks my groin.

"Mmmm," I moan with pleasure.

I open my legs even wider so that he can enter my vagina better
with his tongue.

I feel my muscles contracting. I feel like I'm about to reach my
climax.

Suddenly, he stops licking.

"Damn, what are you doing? I almost came," I said.

He starts laughing.

He continues to lick. He slides his tongue along my groin.

He licks my thighs.

"Please, please, mmmm…"

"I'm almost there; keep going, keep going."

His lips suck harder on my clitoris. I come screaming. I hear how
he swallows my juicy horniness. He licks it completely clean. He
stands up, grabs me by my hips, and pushes his penis deep
inside. He thrusts harder and harder. He wanted to take his penis
out of my vagina, but he couldn't hold it any longer. He squirted
into me.

"That was so hot," he said.

"This is our little secret; don't tell anyone else," I whispered in
his ear.

The same evening, Henry comes to ring the doorbell. He brought
the key to the car. I opened the door.

"Here, ma'am," he said.

"How much should I give you?" I asked Henry.

He looked at me. I leaned against the wall. He closes the door
and stands in front of me. With my right hand, I unbuttoned his
pants, and then my fingers slid over his boxer shorts. I then slid
my hands over his buttocks, squeezing them gently. I felt his

muscles tense. I move my hand forward again, and I feel his penis. I pull down his underwear. I pull hard on his penis.

"Mmm... You feel like it?" I whispered in his ear.

Without saying anything, he pushed his tongue into my mouth. My right hand rested on his shoulders, and he kissed my neck.

"Mm... You smell so good."

He turned me around, lifted my dress, and put the pants on the side. He pushes his penis into my vagina. He starts thrusting. He goes harder and deeper. After fifteen thrusts, he came. Yes, I counted them.

That was fast, I thought.

"You already paid me," he whispers in my ear.

He takes his penis out of my vagina. Pull up his boxer shorts again, close his pants, and walk out the door.

"Your time is up," I say to Denna.

"We will make a follow-up appointment."

Diamantha to readers: "Denna's story will continue in Part 2...Will I see you then?"

Story 4

Do you know that? That you have been in a relationship for years and that the fire has gone out? I was beyond fed up with the situation. It's easy to keep complaining without taking action. Because it's the same bullshit every day. Work, then home. Cooking, eating, and hanging in front of the television until half past ten.

You already know.

It is half past ten. Marc gets up and walks to the bathroom to brush his teeth. I'm tired of his routine. After brushing his teeth, he undresses. He puts the clothes on a chair in the bedroom. Then he crawls under the blanket.

Tonight, I'm going to make a change.

I lie down on his bed. I took his left hand and placed it above his head on the mattress. Furthermore, I grabbed the handcuffs I had hidden under my pillow. I secured his wrists to the bed with the handcuffs.

"What are you doing?" he said in shock.

I put my index finger on his mouth.

"Don't talk; I decide today."

I stand up and smile at him. He looks so hopeless, I thought.

I grabbed the other two cuffs I had left and also secured his legs to the bed.

"Hey, untie me," he says anxiously.

"You look like a starfish now," I told him, laughing.

He is not used to being in a submissive role.

We haven't fucked that often for a while. And when we fuck, it's the same missionary position.

I pulled a box from the bed. I secretly ordered that.

I take out a ball.

I put the ball in his mouth.
"So, now it's time to be zen," I told him.

Now he can't talk or move.
I'm looking for some sensual music.
I slowly take off my clothes. Slowly to the sensual music.
I run my two fingers over my pants. I take a low, thin rod with a
black spring at the end. I teasingly tickled his face with the stick. I
see his penis slowly starting to get hard.
I also started tickling his penis with the wand. His penis jumped. I
took an eye mask from the box and put it on his face. His penis
became harder and harder. Precum comes out of his penis. I
stand up and look at my artwork. I lick away the precum. I pull
my pants aside and sit on him with my face in front of him. I
started riding him.
Even though the ball is still in his mouth, I can hear him moaning.
"Are we going on an adventure? We are going to book Airbnb," I
asked him while I was riding him.
"Mwmmm," he said.
"I don't understand you. Is that a yes?"
I stand up and take the black ball out of his mouth.
"Yes, that seems like a good idea," he said.

And so begins our Airbnb adventure.

"What else have you tried?" I asked Angelina and Marc.

I booked an Airbnb in Florida. It is a luxury apartment next to a
shopping mall.
We walked hand in hand in the shopping mall. We had just come
from a sex shop, where we bought a vibrator with a remote
control.

It's pretty hot to walk around where there are a lot of people, and I have a vibrator in my vagina.

The goal is not to have an orgasm. I'm curious if that will work. Henry controls the remote. Henry had to stay nearby to keep the Bluetooth connection under control. Now and then, I lost control of my legs and collapsed for a moment.
When we got home, the horniness was over, and everything was over. I removed the vibrator from my vagina.
On to something else, I thought.

"We're here," Marc said when he turned on the indicator, and we turned into the driveway of a luxury villa. Marc wanted to surprise me. We get out and take the suitcases out of the car.
"This is going to be a hot week," he said.
The villa was clean and painted white everywhere. Marc opens the door to the garden.
"We have a hot tub in the garden," he shouts at me.
I also went outside to look.
"Don't shout like that. We're in an upscale neighborhood."
"I'll let it warm up."
He grabs my hand and takes me inside. He starts to take off his clothes.
"What are you doing?" I asked him.
"I'm going naked in the hot tube."
"Not me!"
"Come on, don't be so prudish. It's dark, so no one can see us anyway," he said.
I also quickly took off my clothes and followed him.
We sank into the water as deep as we could. I laid my head on the edge of the hot tub. I felt all the stress disappear.
"This is ideal for home," I said to Marc.
I spread my legs and felt the water getting everywhere. It

warmed every part of my body.

I turned around and put my arms over his shoulders.

I gently caressed his cheek.

I pressed my tense nipples against his body. I slowly caressed his upper lip with my tongue.

I put my hand on the back of his neck and ruffled his hair. He looked at me in surprise. I started kneading his chest with my other hand.

"Mmm, what are you doing to me?" he said.

I kiss him on the mouth. I then take his earlobe in my mouth and start sucking gently. Then he puts his fingers in my vagina. It was four fingers, I thought. I start moving up and down on his fingers. I moan loudly.

"Ssssttt, don't moan so loudly."

"Don't stop; I'm cumming now."

I wrapped my hands around his neck and came.

We heard a noise. We looked over and saw that the neighbor was on her upstairs balcony, filming us with her phone.

"So you were caught by the neighbor?" I asked Angelina and Marc.

"Yes, indeed," said Marc.

The next day, I saw the neighbor at the tennis court, and Angelina continued.

"Did you find it hot yesterday when you saw us?" I asked the neighbor.

"Shall we play a game of tennis?" she asked me, without answering my question.

Exhausted, I throw the tennis racket on the tennis court. The neighbor comes to me.

"You're fantastic; congratulations," she said.

"Shall we take a shower?" she asked.

"Yes, that's OK." I got up and walked after her.

There was no one in the locker room; there were two showers next to each other. I take off my clothes while the neighbor looks at me. I took off my sports bra last. I rub my hands over my breasts. I grab my shower stuff from the gym bag and walk to the shower. I feel my neighbor admiring my body with her eyes.

I opened the tap. Put a little shampoo on my hand. I soak my naked, shaven body.

Mmm... How good this feels, I thought.

I use both hands to lubricate my lower legs, upper legs, and calves.

The neighbor comes and stands next to me in the shower. I lube my pussy. I push my labia apart so that the water can reach it better. I pull my legs apart and let the water jets slide down my back into my gluteal cleft.

The neighbor puts her hands on my back.

"Come on, I'll help you rub it in," she says.

I feel her hands exploring my back. I turned around, and she immediately kissed me.

Ooo, her tongue feels so good in my mouth, I thought.

"Is it the first time you have kissed a woman?" I asked Angelina.

"Yes, it was my first time."

I placed my hand on her chest. And I put her nipples between my thumb and forefinger. I squeezed it hard.

"Mmm," she moaned.

Then I massage her breasts with both hands while she starts massaging my pussy. She puts two fingers in my vagina. I start to shake.

"Mmm, what a warm pussy you have," she says.

I feel the muscles of my pussy contracting. She starts fingering my vagina with her fingers while we play a fun game with our tongues. I push two fingers into her vagina. While I massage her clitoris with my thumb. I start moving my fingers faster.

"Mmm, go on mm," she moaned.

We started fingering each other faster and harder until we both came.

The next day, we went to a Wellness Centre. We got a massage, manicure, and pedicure. After my adventure with the neighbor, I wanted to try new things again.

When I got home, Marc was upstairs in bed. He was watching television.

"Are you nice and naked in bed?" I asked him.

"Yes, come lie with me," he said.

I take off my clothes and lie down next to him.

"What do you think of my feet."

He feels my feet.

"It feels nice and soft."

"Shall I massage you with it?" I asked.

"What do you mean?"

"My feet are clean, and my nails are trimmed, so don't worry," I said.

I get up and take coconut oil from my bag.

"What is that for?" he asked.

"It's for my foot. It makes the skin extra soft."

I sit opposite him. I caress his upper body with my feet. He grabs my foot and sucks on my toes. Then I put my wet toes on his penis, teasingly. I wiggle in his most sensitive spot.

How special this is, I thought.

He grabs my foot again and starts massaging the soles of my feet with his thumbs.

"Mmm, it's so wonderful," I moaned.

I then put coconut oil on the soles of my feet. I place his penis between my soles and rub up and down. I'm going faster and faster.

"Mmm... What are you doing to me?", he moaned.

I place my feet on the narrow edge behind the penis head.

"Do you know what that's called?" I asked Angelina.

"No"

"It's called Frenulum."

"It's a very sensitive part of a glans. So the perfect place to touch with your toes."

I rest his penis on his stomach. I gently tap my toes on the Frenulum. Then I stroked my biggest toe against it, up and down. He stood on the bed with his penis against the sole of my foot. He started moving up and down.

"I, I, I," Marc groaned.

He came on the sole of my foot.

"How do the footjobs feel?" I asked Marc.

"It feels better than the hand job. The feeling of softly oiled feet around your penis. Mmmm... Nice. It feels like the softest, smoothest vagina. Looking at beautiful feet. I'm very attracted to feet at the moment. She has made me addicted to her footjobs. I can enjoy it for hours. A 10-minute footjob feels like hours of fucking. And when I cum on it...mmmm it's wonderfully liberating."

"That shouldn't be a problem," I said.

Diamantha to readers:" The story of Angelina and Marc will be continued in Part 2 of the book. Will I see you then?"

Story 5

The time has finally come. I have arrived at the camping. Packing things, loading the car, and forgetting anything is always a challenge.

When you arrive at the camp, you immediately unload your belongings and set up the tent.

The first day is always resting from the journey.

The next day, I went for a bike ride. I came across a quiet beach. It was a perfect place to see the sunset. I get some food and drinks from my bag. I certainly didn't forget my blanket and camera. It was still wonderfully warm. I find it strange that I'm sitting here alone.

Don't the other people at the camping know where to find this beach? I thought.

In the distance, I see someone walking towards me. As I got closer, I saw that a beautiful blonde woman was in her early 20s. She has long, curly hair.

"Nice," she said.

She shook my hand.

"India".

"Bernard, nice."

She sat down next to me.

"I've been coming here almost every day since I moved here; do you live around here too?" she asked.

"No, I'm here for two weeks. I find camping very relaxing. Nice two weeks in nature," I said.

"Do you want something to drink?", I asked.

"No, thanks"

She quickly gets up and takes off her clothes and shoes. She quickly ran to the sea and took a dip.

"Are you coming too?" she asked as she came up.

You don't have to ask me twice, I thought.

I quickly took off my clothes and shoes. And I also ran to the sea and took a dip.

"It's so cold," I said.

"You get used to it," she says.

She started splashing me, and I started running after her.

"I got you," I said as I grabbed her.

She put her arms around me and gave me an intense kiss. I felt my penis start to grow because of this. That did not go unnoticed. She grabbed my penis with her hand.

"Mmm," I moaned.

She moved her hands back and forth.

What an unexpected erotic experience this is, I thought.

She put her legs around my hip.

I felt something warm. Yes, that was her vagina.

Wow, what a combination of a cold sea and warm vagina. With that feeling, I started thrusting harder.

Wow, how the waves move with my penis.

Wow, every moan with every thrust.

Mmm, better than any vibrator.

I couldn't hold it back anymore. We came at the same time.

The next day, I sat around a campfire with other neighbors from the camping. We were enjoying drinks and music. Everyone went to sleep. Me, Robin, and Melinda stayed behind. I put the last logs on the fire.

"It's hot," Melinda said. She takes off her T-shirt and picks up a bottle of wine that is on the floor.

"Who wants wine?"

Before we could say anything, she filled our glasses. She puts the wine back on the floor. She walks towards us again and takes my hand. Furthermore, she grabs Robin's hand with the other hand.

She guides our hands to her breasts. We hold her breasts while she takes off her bra.

"Take your hands away for a moment," she says.

She dropped the bra on the floor.

Wow, what nice big breasts with big nipples, I thought. I immediately felt like sucking it.

She walks over to me, grabs my hands, puts them on her breasts, and kisses me on my cheek. Then she goes to Robin. She grabs his hands, puts them on her breasts, and kisses him on the mouth.

I felt myself starting to get excited. She turned and started kissing me while Robin's hands were still on her breasts.

She stood up.

"Stand up," she ordered.

We stood up. She sat down on a chair.

"Come stand before me."

"Take off your clothes. One by one. And to the rhythm of the music."

We did exactly what she asked.

At the same time, she started to jerk us off gently with her hand. She put our penis in her mouth.

She stood up. She took off her pants and underwear. Not only that, but she pushes Robin onto the chair she was previously sitting on. She sat on him. She put his penis in her vagina and started riding him.

I enjoy the view.

"Play with yourself," she commanded.

I started playing with myself.

"Come here."

She put my penis in her mouth while she was riding Robin.

She started riding faster and sucking harder. After a while, all three of us came at the same time.

"What's wrong with your experience?", I asked Bernard.

"Well," he continued.

It was the last day. Everyone was packing. I went to help Donna with her tent.
"Thanks for helping with the tent," she said.
"Where is your car? I can help you pack," I said to her.
"I came by Uber. I'm going to call the Uber in a moment."
"I can take you."
"That's very sweet of you," she said.
It was around three o'clock when we finished packing the car.
After four hours of driving, we decided to take a break.
I parked my car where it was dark, so no one could see us when we peed.
Donna was the first to pee between the trees. When she came back, I went to pee.
When I came back, I saw that she had put her pants on the handlebars. I got behind the wheel again.
"It will be fun like this," I told her. She kisses me in the mouth. I grabbed her head and gave her an intense kiss. She kissed her way over the handbrake and sat on my lap. I move my chair further back so she has more space. I immediately felt something warm.
Yes, that was her vagina. I put my hands on her hips. She moved her hips up and down.
We both started to moan. I leaned back with my hands on her breasts. While she moves back and forth, I massage her breasts with my hands.
"Come on, let's go to the back seat. I'm going to fuck you deep," I told her.

She takes off her dress and bra. I gave her a push on her
buttocks, which made her climb back easily. I also climbed back.
Furthermore, I sat down and took off my pants and underwear.
She kneels in front of me, takes my penis into her mouth, and
starts sucking it. I put my hand on her head and pushed her head
down so she could go deeper.
She takes my penis out of her mouth and starts sucking my balls.
"Mmm, how nice."
I started jerking off with my hand.
"I'm going to fuck you again," I said.
I pushed her forward so she was leaning on her knees and
hands. I put my hands on her hips and pushed my penis deep
into her.
"AAA"
We both moaned at the same time. I started thrusting hard.
With each thrust, I smacked her buttocks. Faster and faster,
harder and harder, until I couldn't do it anymore. She came first.
I pushed her up with her back against my chest.
"I'm not done with you yet," I said.
I pressed her against the back railing so she could look out the
back window. I put my penis back in her vagina and started
thrusting again, but this time slowly. I put my thumb on her
clitoris and started going in circles. She came again.
"Come on, come on."
She started to moan and came again. Her wetness made me
hornier, and I started thrusting harder.
I moaned and came too.
I plopped into the backseat. She licked my penis clean and
started sucking again.
"Isn't it fair to cum again?" she said.
She starts licking my cock. She goes a lot further down, quickly

comes back up, and takes my penis in her mouth again.
How delicious this is, I thought.

I moaned loudly and put my hand on her head to make her go deeper. She moved her head deeper, making me moan again. I couldn't hold it anymore and filled her throat.
"I knew you were a slut," she said.

"I notice you're still enjoying that moment. Then why are you sitting here?" I asked Bernard.

Diamantha to readers: "Bernard's story continues in Part 2. Will I see you then?"

Story 6

I'm lying comfortably on the couch. From the living room, I can
see how the technician is working in the kitchen.
What muscular arms he has, I thought. I notice that I'm getting
hornier.
This morning I had sex with my husband. How can I still be
horny?
He has a big heart on his right arm.
Oh, he's in love, I thought.
But should I watch it or not?
He wipes sweat from his forehead and takes off his T-shirt.
Well, I'm not the only one feeling hot, I thought.
Oh, he's so muscular. It's wide. He has triceps and biceps. I hope
it's big and wide down there too.
He gets a call.
I hope it's not his wife.
He walks towards me.
"Ma'am, I just received a call from a colleague. I have to help him
with an urgent job. I will come and finish the work tomorrow."
Will you come and kill me tomorrow too? I thought.
"Yes, that's no problem. Will it be finished tomorrow?" I asked
him.
"Yes, I will finish it tomorrow."
He puts on his T-shirt and walks away.
Too bad, I can't enjoy the view anymore. Tomorrow is another
new day.

The next morning, I opened the door. I'm still in my bathrobe.
And yes, I'm not wearing anything. My husband just left. And
yes, we had a nice fuck before that. We are extra horny with this
warm weather. I still smell of cum.

I open the bathrobe and put two fingers in my vagina.
Furthermore, I started fingering myself in front of the technician.
"Are you still coming in, or are you going to stay there and
watch?" I asked him.
He comes in and closes the door.
He takes my hand. Together, we walked to the dining room. He
takes a chair. He takes off his clothes and sits on the chair.
"Come stand here in front of me," he says.
"Continue masturbating."
I put my fingers in my vagina again and continued masturbating.
He looks at me while also playing with himself. His penis also
starts to get big and hard.
Exactly what I thought. It's also big and wide.
"Mmm... You are such a naughty lady," he says.
"Mmm... Come and sit on this."
I sit on his lap. He pushes his penis deep into me.
"Ooo..."
"That's nice, that lovely big cock of yours," I said.
I started moving up and down. I sit back, and he starts playing
with my clitoris. He starts giving short thrusts aimed at my G-
spot.
Mmm... What a wonderful combination!

***"That's called the Reclined Lap Dance 180," I say to Monique.
"Continue with your story."***

"Get up."
I stood up, and so did he.
He grabs my neck with one hand and pulls me towards him.
He gives me a fiery kiss.
"I want you deep inside me," I told him.

I lay down on the floor with my legs up over my head, and I lift my lower back off the ground.
He squats over my head while leaning forward, pushing his penis deep into my vagina.

"Do you know what that position is called?" I asked Monique.
"No".
"That's a form of Pile Driver Position. I think maybe it's the Twisted variant," I said to Monique.
"But move on."

He massages my clitoris while he is inside me.
That's a double pleasure.
He takes his penis out of my vagina and pushes his tongue into my vagina.
I enjoy his tongue in my vagina. He goes in and out with his tongue.
"I'm almost there."
He moves his tongue faster and faster. In and out. In and out.
I squirted. His face and mouth were full of my cum. I sat up and licked his face clean.
"Mmm, you taste so good," he said.
He stood up and pushed his penis deep into my throat.
He fucked my mouth. Not only that, but he went deeper and deeper into my throat. In and out of my mouth. Deeper and deeper in and out. Then I felt a very warm juice in my mouth. He screamed in pleasure.
I swallowed everything.
"That was hot and delicious. Would you like something to drink before you start to work?" I asked him.

"Could he have finished his job as he promised? Next time we will talk about Alex, the technician."

Diamantha to readers: More about Alex in Part 2!

Story 7

Can you imagine that I took swimming lessons as an adult?

I was looking for relaxation and to keep up my fitness. I thought, Why not combine all three?

Learn something, relax, improve your fitness, and lose weight. So four things.

After work, I never have time to go home first to get dressed and to eat something. So I eat a sandwich at work, and then I change clothes. Beats rushing three times a week.

There are eight of us between twenty and forty years old. Five women and three men. One of those guys is as tall as me. His name is Tony.

I go not only to swim but also to watch him.

His presence alone makes me horny. I don't think he noticed that.

I always behave properly. Not only that, I am a decent woman.

I've already changed at work, so I just have to take off my clothes and put them in my bag. I put the bag in a locker and walked to the pool.

I'm just in time. Everyone has already jumped into the swimming pool. I also jump into the swimming pool.

While swimming, the swimming instructors watch us to see if we have mastered swimming techniques properly.

Tony came swimming next to me.

"Hey, you were almost late today," Tony said.

"Yes, I had to work overtime today."

"Faster," shouts the swimming instructor.

After swimming for thirty minutes, the swimming lesson ended.

I'm glad it's thirty minutes. You'll be completely exhausted when you're done.

I get out of the pool and walk towards the locker. I get my bag
from the locker and walk to a separate shower room. I hang up
my bag and take the shampoo and shower cream out of the bag.
I put them on the floor and turned on the shower.
Mmm, how wonderful. Some time for myself after a long day at
work, I thought.
Tony comes inside and locks the door. He stands behind me.
Shit, didn't I lock the door? I thought.
"Is it my idea, or do you fancy me too?" he whispered in my ear.
"I ... I," I stuttered.
I feel my breathing quicken.
He moves his body more against me.
"Do you feel that too?"
I feel his penis against my ass.
"Yes, I feel something. What is that?"
He takes off his swimming trunks and comes back to me.
"Does that feel better?"
"Wow, yes, I feel it."
I turn around, and he kisses me fervently.
I grab his buttocks and squeeze them. He bites my lip and pushes
his tongue into my mouth again.
He turns me around and presses me against the wall. He puts a
hand against the wall. With the other hand, he explores my
body. He caresses my breasts. He slowly goes down towards my
belly button. He puts a finger on my belly button. He kisses my
neck. He continues down with his hand. He stops at my pussy.
"Does me make you horny?" he whispered in my ear.
"Go on," I said.
He grabs my hips and pushes his penis deep into my vagina. I
was shocked and groaned.
"Not so loud; otherwise, other people will notice us," he said.
This felt so intense.

This felt so intimate.

He takes his penis out completely. And then again, deep into my vagina.

He squeezes my buttocks. He goes up and down. Up and down. In and out.

"I wanted you from the first day I saw you," he whispered in my ear as he moved in and out of me.

"That feels so, so, so…"

I couldn't finish my sentence. I couldn't hold back anymore and came. I open my legs and grab his buttocks with my hands.

"Fuck me deeper, go deeper."

He goes deeper with his penis. I came again.

"Are you coming again?" he asked.

"Yes, yes, don't stop."

He starts panting more and more heavily.

We move together at his pace. He feels that I have come again.

"Come on, baby. Come on."

He takes his penis out of my vagina.

"Why are you doing that? I hadn't come yet," I said.

"Me neither."

He puts his penis in me again. He picks up the pace again. After a few hard thrusts, he came. He takes his penis out of my vagina.

"The bodyguard," I say to Eva.

"The Bodyguard?", Eva asked Diamantha

"Yes, that's what the position is called, The Bodyguard. That's the simple version of it.

"Have you been caught, or have people heard you?" I asked Eva.

Diamantha to readers: "Are you also curious? See you in Part 2."

Story 8

That's what we are there for as parents. My child forgot his book at school and has an exam the next day.

I quickly went to his school to pick up his book.

Once at school, it was very quiet. All the children have already gone home. I only see a few cleaners walking around.

I open the classroom and see no one.

The teacher has already gone home, I thought.

I heard some footsteps in the hallway. I secretly took shelter in the closet.

Why would I hide in a closet? I'm not doing anything wrong, am I? I thought.

The classroom door opens and closes. I open the cupboard door a little.

I see Director Martin kissing the teacher.

Furthermore, I carefully take the phone out of my pocket and start filming.

What I see makes me soaking wet.

He opens her blouse and unhooks her bra.

"Wow, she has beautiful nipples," I whispered.

He takes her left nipple in his mouth while he massages her right nipple with his other hand. He sucks her nipples hard.

She moaned.

"SSsshhh, not so hard. We'll get caught soon," Martin says to Ariana.

She puts her hands under his t-shirt and takes it off.

"Wow, he has such a beautifully toned body," I whispered.

She pulls down his pants and pulls down his underwear. She runs her hand up and down his cock.

He groaned.

"Not so hard, or we'll get caught, remember!", says Ariana.
I feel myself getting wetter and wetter.

He picks her up, puts her on her desk, and then pushes his penis
into her vagina.
Both moan.
He starts thrusting into her slowly. He's going faster and faster.
I'm so excited. I put my hand in my pants while I film them with
my phone in the other hand.
I stop filming and put my phone back in my pocket. At that
moment, the door of the cupboard opens further.
"Shit."
I'm busted!
Both are shocked. We looked at each other for a moment in fear.
I walked towards them.
"Go on," I said.
He thrusts into her hard.
I put my hands in my pants and start masturbating while I look at
them.
I'm cumming. Furthermore, I put two fingers in my vagina. I feel
how wet my vagina is. I take those fingers out of my vagina and
put them in his mouth.
"You taste so good," he says.
I start caressing her. I close my eyes. Not only that, but I feel her
hands on my breasts.
I take off my T-shirt. She pulls my nipples.
"Mmm..." I moaned.
"Come here," he said.
He grabs my neck and starts kissing me as he thrusts into her
hard.
He takes his penis out of Ariana's vagina.
He puts three fingers in my vagina.
"Oh, you're so wet," he said.

"Take off your pants."

I take off my pants.

"Bend down for me, so I can see you."

He then slaps me on my butt. He puts his penis in my vagina. He goes deeper and deeper. I bend over and touch the floor.

"Oo, this is so deep," I moaned.

Ariana enjoys our fuck while masturbating.

He grabs my hips and thrusts harder and deeper.

He takes his penis out of my vagina.

"Will you kneel before me with your mouths open?"

Ariana and I sat in front of him with our heads together and our mouths wide open.

"Ooo, … Here he comes. Here he comes," he moaned.

He filled our mouths and faces completely.

"Downward Doggy, how wonderful that is," I say to Iris.

"Down…What?" says Iris.

"Downward Doggy is what it is called. It is a variant of the popular Doggystyle. You both stand while the woman bends over and touches the ground. As a woman, you can also bend at the knees. It offers a lot of stimulation to the vagina. It also offers stimulation of the man's glans. Not only that, but it is one of my favorites," I say to Iris.

Story 9

I knocked on the door.

"Room service," I said.

I got no response, so I opened the door.

I take the sheets off the bed. I hear the bathroom door open.

I turn around and see a tall man in a suit.

We looked deeply into each other's eyes without saying anything.

"I knocked, but no one answered."

"I didn't hear it. I have my earplugs in," he said.

He kept looking at me. It felt so uncomfortable.

"Do you mind if I continue with my work?" I asked him.

"No, that's no problem," he said, laughing.

I moved on to the sheets.

"Here tonight at ten o'clock," he whispered in my ear and walked out of the room.

What does he think I am?, I thought.

What ten o'clock? What am I doing here at ten o'clock? I've already finished work.

What does he think I am? I'm not a whore!

It's three o'clock, and I'm done with work. After meeting him, I was so angry.

Once home, I collapsed on the couch.

"What a day."

He was a nice, attractive man. You can see from his clothes that he has money.

If only I had a man like him as my partner. Then I never have to work again. I will never have to clean again. Will it be cleaned for me?

I think and think. Should I go anyway?

Every day, it's the same: work at home. Home to work.
Mmm, maybe I should make a change today, I thought.
I jump off the couch and walk to the bedroom. I open the
wardrobe door.
"What should I wear?" I was thinking.
I grab a black dress, a black bra, and a black thong and put them
on the bed. I grab a wig and put it on the bed too.
"I don't want to be recognized by my colleagues."
I walk to the bathroom. I removed the hair under my armpits
and on my pubic hair.
Then I take a hot shower.
I get dressed, put on some makeup, and put on the wig.
"I'm ready for the horny adventure."
I pack my bag and leave home.
I walk to work. Once there, I look at my phone. I have three
minutes left.
There I am. I knocked on the door once. I feel the adrenaline in
my body.
He opens the door and looks at me. He's only wearing boxers.
"Turn around," he said.
I turned around.
"What a nice ass you have," he said, and he slapped me on the
ass.
He pulls me in by the hand.
He grabs my buttocks and pushes my lower body against his.
"You are such a beautiful and horny woman. Tonight is all about
me," he said, giving me a French kiss.
I sit on the edge of the bed and pull him towards me.
"What are you going to do?" he asked.
He takes off his boxers. I hold his cock with my hand and put it in
my mouth.

Mmm, he moaned.

He takes a step back.

Get on your knees with your back to me. He sits behind me, also kneeling, resting on his calves. He puts his penis in my vagina and starts thrusting with his pelvis.

I start rocking back and forth.

This is crazy, I thought.

"Oo, baby," he moaned.

He keeps thrusting, and I also keep moving my pelvis.

"Come and lie on your back," he said.

I lay down on my back. He just raises my left leg and puts his penis in my vagina. He crosses my thigh over his body and continues thrusting.

"Do you like it?" he groaned.

He puts his finger on my clitoris while he's thrusting.

"Wow, wow, you're so hot, hot," he moaned.

He takes out his penis. He grabs my legs and raises them both. Furthermore, he puts his penis in me again.

"Oh, you're so nice and deep inside me," I moaned.

I wrap my legs around his hips. I determine the rhythm with my legs.

"I'm almost here," he said.

"Wait for me first," I said. He started thrusting harder, so I came. I hugged him and came hard.

He took his penis out of my vagina. I sat down. He stood on the bed and put his penis in my mouth.

"Ooo, what a delightful mouth you have," he moaned, and he put his penis deeper in my mouth. In the meantime, I massage his balls with my hands. Rhythmically, he starts fucking my mouth. In and out. In and out.

"Mmm," I moaned.

"I want to get between your breasts," he said.

I lie down on the bed with my head hanging over the foot of the bed. He sits on top of me and pushes his hard penis between my big, soft breasts. I press my breasts against his penis with both hands. He moves back and forth. Every time his penis comes near my mouth, I give his glans a lick. He moves his penis faster between my breasts.

"I'm coming," he moaned. A whole load came between my breasts. He puts his penis in my mouth, and I suck out the last drop.

"My name is Carlos, by the way," he said, panting.

He takes his penis out of my mouth and falls contentedly onto the bed.

"Isabella," I said, laughing.

"The first position is called Lazy Doggy. You can also place pillows underneath your knees if you want to try it on the floor," I said

"The second position is called Twisted Kneeling Scissors," I say.

"I have no idea what it's called, but I loved it," Isabella said.

"You did a great job in the third position. At Wrapped Missionary, you decided how he was going to punch," I said, laughing.

"He thought he had the power over me all day," Isabella said, laughing.

"And then?", I asked Isabella.

To be continued in Part 2!

Story 10

After a bad relationship breakup, I decided to finally do
something crazy in my life.
I went on a trip to South America alone. Everyone called me
crazy, but I did it anyway.
It would be dangerous on my own, but you live once in a while.
I went to Chapada Diamantha in Brazil. I didn't feel like going
with a large group, so I hired a private guide.

The weather was beautiful. The sun shines wonderfully on my
bare arms. It was so hot that I wanted to walk around naked. But
that's not possible because you don't know who you'll meet.
"Hi, I'm João," he said.
"Hi, Sophie."
"Shall we start our journey right away? There is so much to
experience."
We walked through the park for hours. It has a very beautiful
nature. You immediately feel the peace. Nature is the only place
where you can find that peace.
Finally! We have reached our goal, the mountain of Morro do Pai
Inacio. What a beautiful view. It is bizarre that this exists. Not
only is the view beautiful, but the guide is also a gem of a guy.
He is a muscular man, with wide arms, sturdy legs, and a nice-
shaped ass.
I feel like squeezing his ass.
"What a beautiful view," I said.
"Yes, like you," he said, giving me a wink.
What did I hear? I thought.
"Shall we continue walking?" he said.
We walked further.

I noticed that I was starting to get wet. Not wet from rain, no.
His comment made me wet.

We arrived at a small lake.
"It's bright blue, very nice."
"You can jump in if you want," he said.
Without hesitation, I took off my clothes and jumped naked into
the lake.
"What are you doing? A lot of people come here," he said.
"But now there are no people," I replied.
He looked around to make sure there weren't any people
around.
"Okay, I'll come save you," he said.
"To rescue?" I said, laughing.
He also took off his clothes and jumped into the water.
My heart starts beating faster when he starts swimming near
me. I tried to swim away, but he grabbed my leg and pulled me
towards him.
Where are you going? I came to save you, right? "He said.
We looked at each other for a while. Without saying anything.
I closed my eyes. And no, it's not a dream. I felt his mouth on my
mouth. I felt something big against my legs. And no, it's not a
fish.
I opened my mouth, so his tongue could play with my tongue.
He turned me and stood behind me. I felt his penis against my
ass.
" Nice huh"
"Yes, beautiful," I said. But I have no idea what he means.
He kisses me on the neck. He puts his left hand on my right
breast. With his right hand, he massages my clitoris.
I moan with pleasure.
"Can you feel him against your ass?" he asked.
"Uhhhh", I groaned.

He moves back and forth between my ass and his penis.
"I can't take it anymore; I'm going to fuck you."

He turned me around and pushed his penis deep into me in one go.
"Oh, Que gostos."
The water moves with every thrust.
Up and down, up and down.
"Oh, que gostos," I said back.
I leaned back into a dip position so he could go deeper.
He puts his arms around me.
We heard footsteps.
We quickly stopped fucking and ran out of the lake.
"Come on, quick. Quick! I don't want to lose my job," he said.
We quickly grabbed our clothes and took shelter behind a large rock.
We quickly got dressed before people got to the lake.
Once dressed, we walked on secretly.
"Are you okay?" he asked.
"Yes, it's okay. But it's a shame we couldn't go any further," I said.
"I know a place where it is quieter."
We arrive at a place that is quite wooded.
"Wow, it's so beautiful here. All those different types of plants and trees."
"Yes, it's a good place to pick up where we left off," he says.
He grabs my neck and gives me a passionate kiss.
This was a good opportunity for me to squeeze his ass.
I put my hands on his buttocks and squeezed them hard.
"Mmm," he moaned.
I press him against my body. I feel that he has gotten an erection again.
Not only that, but I turn around quickly. Furthermore, I open my

pants and pull my pants down to my knee. And bends down to
him.

"Fuck me, fuck me. Now!" I said.

He also takes down his pants and boxers and puts his penis back
in my vagina.

We both moaned in pleasure with each thrust. Every in and out.
Until his last thrust.

"Que gostooossoo," so we came at the same time.

He got on his knees with his face in front of my ass. He grabs my
ass cheeks with his hand and pulls them apart.

"Mmmm...," I moaned.

I felt his tongue at my asshole. He licks my asshole.

What is this? I thought.

He licks my asshole faster. He moves very quickly.

"Ohh, what a talent! Ohh, how nice."

I came.

Wait, did I come from his tongue near my asshole? I wondered.

I was astounded.

He stood up and kissed me in the mouth.

Secretly, I thought it was dirty but also horny.

*"That's called Anilingus. That means you stimulate the anus
with your tongue," I say to Sophie.*

"Ana...What?"

"Anilingus is a Latin word for rimming," I say.

*"And the first time you had sex with him. Do you know what
that position is called?" I asked.*

"No".

*"It's called Dipping Dancer. It provides a better angle for
penetration."*

"Are you still in touch with him? Have you met up after that

tour?" I asked.

Diamantha to readers: "Are you also curious? Wait for part 2!"

Story 11

"His dream is my worst nightmare."
He fantasized about it. He wanted it so bad. Like a good wife, I
went along with it.

Every Wednesday, the children go to stay with their
grandmother. We wait for this day every week to finally be
intimate with each other. Wednesday fuck day is on our agenda.

"Hey, babe, I'm on my way home. Looking forward to it tonight,"
he had said.
I went to the bedroom and grabbed a black box that was on the
cupboard. I put the box on the bed and opened it. In the box, we
have everything: handcuffs, whips, dildos, and lube. It's our sex
box.
What should we try today? I thought.
My eyes fall on the strap-on.
"Mmm, let's try this one out," I said, smiling.
I immediately felt that I was starting to get excited. I take the
strap-on out of the box and put it on. I stood in front of the
mirror and took a picture of it with my phone.
I'll send that photo to Eric.
"That doesn't look good with clothes on."
I take off my clothes, leaving only my bra and pants on.
I put the strap-on on my pants.
I stand in front of the mirror again.
"That looks better. And hot."
I hold the penis and stroke it.
"I'm going to spoil Eric today."
I felt horny, and I also felt powerful. It's wonderful that I'm in
charge today.
I loosen the strap a bit so that I can easily reach my briefs. I put

my hand in my pants. I reach my clitoris with my fingers.

I start masturbating myself with the strap-on on.

"Mmm….. How horny I get from the thought that I'm going to fuck Eric today. How horny, the power makes me… mm mm."

I ran my fingers over my clitoris faster until I came.

I heard the front door of the house close.

I take an eye mask out of the box and quickly put it back in the cupboard.

I put the eye mask on the bed.

"Nadia, I'm home," Eric shouts.

"I'm in the bedroom. Take a shower right away and wait for me in the bedroom. Lie naked on the bed," I told him.

Eric immediately walks to the bathroom. While he was showering, I opened the door a little so he couldn't see the strap-on.

"When you're done, lie down on the bed and put on the eye mask," I told him.

"Oo… how exciting! What are you planning?" he asked.

"You'll find out soon."

I took shelter in a children's room.

Eric did exactly as I said. He lay naked on the bed and put on the eye mask.

"I'm in bed," he shouted.

I walk to our bedroom and put on some exciting music. I have now taken off the strap-on.

I place the strap-on next to him on the bed and sit in front of his mouth.

"Open your mouth. Take out the tongue."

I pressed my pussy against his lips.

"Lick me. Make me come."

I pull my labia apart with my hands so that my clitoris can be licked properly.

I started moving my body back and forth while he was licking
me.
"Mmmm," I moaned.
"Go faster with the tongue."
He started moving his tongue faster.
"I'm cumming. I I..."
I sprayed his face all over.
I stood up.
"Now I'm going to show you who's the boss," I said to him.
"Put your knees up a little."
I gently insert a finger into his anus and move towards his belly
button.
I remove my finger from his anus again. I put a little lubricant on
my finger, and then I put it back in his anus. I gently ease my
finger deeper. I felt a small bulge.
"You know what I feel," I said.
"No."
"I feel your prostate."
I started to gently massage his prostate with my finger.
"Do you like this?", I asked him.
"Yes, nice. Keep going," he said.
I continued massaging gently. His penis started to get harder and
harder.
While my finger is in his ass, I take his penis into my mouth. I
start sucking his penis.
"Mmm..." he moaned.
"What are you doing to me, baby?".
"I'm almost here," he said.
I quickly remove his penis from my mouth and also remove my
finger from his anus.
"Not so fast. I decide when that will happen," I said.
"Get on your hands and knees," I said.

I put on the strap-on.

I push his head and shoulders against the bed.

"Put your butt up a little."

I took some lubricant and spread it between his buttocks. I push a finger into his ass. I move my finger back and forth. I take the finger out of his ass. I put lubricant on two fingers and pushed those fingers into his ass. I move my fingers back and forth again.

"You think that's hot?" I asked.

"It doesn't feel bad," he said.

I take the fingers out of his ass. I put lubricant on four fingers and put all four in his ass.

"Aaa, not so fast."

"Does it hurt?" I asked him.

"A little; I just need to get used to it."

I didn't move my fingers for two seconds.

"I think my fingers have spoiled your ass enough."

I take my fingers out of his ass.

I put lubricant on the strap-on.

I just need to rub it in really well, I thought.

"Come closer to the edge of the bed," I told him.

I then stood behind him and pushed the tip in a little.

"Wow, what is that?" he asked.

"You'll find out soon."

I now insert the strap-on into him in one go. I stand still. I'm not moving.

"Careful, babe," he said.

"Today I am the boss. I decided that," I said sternly.

I remove the strap-on from his ass again. This time, I put the strap-on deep.

Wow, I'm fucking him. This feels so hot, I thought.

"Put your hands behind your back," I said.

I grab his hands and move my hips faster.

"How do you feel, babe? Are you going to be nice to me?"
"Yes, babe. I'm going to be nice to you," he said.
"Yes? After four thrusts, you can come."
"Can you do that?" I asked him.
"Yes, I'm going to come for you."
"Can I come now, babe?"
"Yes, come on, come on."
He started jerking off. After four seconds, he came hard.

"You gave him a good prostate massage," I said to Nadia.
"Prostate massage?" Nadia asked.
"Yes, you can reach the gland by, for example, putting a finger in the butt. By massaging the prostate, you prevent bacteria from accumulating. Men can experience a more intense orgasm than a normal orgasm."
"I noticed that, Yes!" Nadia said.
"But why do you say it's your worst nightmare?" I asked Nadia.

Diamantha to readers:" Are you also curious? Follow book 2!"

Story 12

My husband and I are both lawyers. You can understand. Busy, busy, busy, and especially with a small child.

Sometimes I have days when I feel like doing nothing.

No husband, no child, no work. Just nothing at all.

It's a rush every day. It's a performance every day.

Today I have to go to a hearing on the other side of the country with a client. I have decided to stay at a hotel. For both of us, it was impossible to travel six hours back and forth.

From day 1, I felt a special tension between us. I get wet just looking at him.

Since giving birth, I feel different. I don't get turned on by my husband like I used to. They say that a child would be good for your relationship, but that is not the case with me.

My pussy feels different after giving birth. I do not know what it is. I can't explain it very well.

What I do know is that this client, Sebastian, makes my heart beat again.

It feels nice to forget my responsibilities at home for a moment. I call it escaping from the home prison.

"Hello, this is Sebastian."

"Hey, where are you? I've been waiting in the bar for a while."

"I'm on my way. We're still thirty minutes late."

"Okay, I'll walk to the room. It's number 306. It's hectic.

Everything is full, so we have to share a room. We do have two separate beds," I said to Sebastian.

"Okay, that's no problem. I hope I don't wake you up with my snoring," he said.

You can wake me up for something else, I thought hornily.

"No, I hope it's not that bad. I'll see you later, then," I said and hung up.

I enter the elevator and press three.

Once in the room, I take off my clothes and take a warm bath. I put on some relaxing music.

After a while, I hear someone knocking on the door. I quickly got out of the bath and put on a bathrobe that was in the wardrobe. I open the door. Yep, there he is.

Sebastian comes in and closes the door behind him.

"Sorry, I was late," he said.

"You cannot help it."

I was taking a nice bath.

"I think I'll take a nice bath too."

"I'm going to put on my clothes now, so you can get in."

"We can also go in together," he said, laughing.

"No, that's not allowed. That's unprofessional," I said.

I took my pajamas out of my bag, then my vibrator fell out of the bag.

I looked at him shamefully. He gave me a wink.

I quickly put the vibrator in the suitcase and walked to the bathroom in my pajamas.

I put on my clothes and opened the door again.

"I'm done; you can take a bath now," I told him.

"I know this is very unprofessional. But..."

He grabs me, pushes me against the wall, and kisses me.

"Can I help you with anything? I can help you with your vibrator."

"And how is the gentleman going to help me?" I said, laughing.

He grabs my throat and pushes his tongue into my mouth.

We started playing a game with our tongues.

I started to moan with pleasure.

He stops.

"Can I continue?" he asked as he ran his hand over my body.

He slides his hand over my buttocks and squeezes it hard.

I groaned.

He then slides his hands over my breasts. Then he slides his hands back down between my legs. He pulls my pants to the side so he can reach my clitoris.

"Mmmm…" I moaned.

He kisses me passionately again.

What am I doing? I thought.

I pushed him away.

"This is not possible. I cannot do erotic or sexual things with a client. This will cost me my career. And not only my career but also my family. I love my husband."

He takes down his pants. I saw something I'd never seen before in my life.

You shouldn't generalize, but it would be true what they say about black men, I thought.

"Are you sure you don't want it?" he asked, looking at his hard megapenis.

That's better than my vibrator, I thought.

He comes close to my ear.

"I can give you hours of pleasure," he whispered in my ear.

I felt my cheeks turn red.

I felt my pussy getting wet. But I can't tell him that. I can't let him know that I want him more after seeing his megapenis.

He grabs my hand and guides it to his megapenis.

"I know you want him."

I grab his penis and squeeze it.

"Ouch, be careful with it."

"It's better than a vibrator, you think?"

"I'm sure."

We looked at each other for a moment without saying anything.

Will you take the risk, Emma? I asked myself.

I felt an intense sensation come over me. This feeling is new to me.
I push him onto the bed.
"Sit with your hands bent back," I told him. I sat on him.
"Open your legs and bend them a little," I told him.
I put his hard penis in my vagina and leaned back in a crab position. I started moving my hips quickly.
"Ow...This is so good," I moaned.
Sebastian also moaned in pleasure.
I stood up and pushed him back.
"Lie down," I said.
I kneel in front of him, and I lick his cock.
He groans.
I put his penis in my mouth, but it doesn't quite fit in my mouth. It's that big and thick.
I sucked his cock hard.
"Mmmm..." he moaned.
I feel my pussy getting wetter.
"Wait, grab your vibrator, and play with yourself while you suck me," he says.
I did exactly what he asked.
"Stop," he said.
I stopped, and he stood up.
"Come on, sit on that chair."
I sat down on the chair, and he bent down in front of me. He grabs my legs. Each hand holds a leg.
Then look at me. I was on a chair with my legs spread as far sideways as possible. And I'm being deeply penetrated by a client's megapenis, I thought.
Ooo, it couldn't be hotter and naughtier.
He goes so deep with his penis in me.

"Ooo, GOOODDD," I shouted.

He goes deeper and deeper. He's going faster and faster.

I feel an orgasm. I felt myself shaking.

"Come on, babe. Come on," he moaned.

"I am coming." I feel my muscles contracting. I have never come so hard before.

He quickly removes his penis from my vagina and sprays my stomach full of his cum.

"The first position is called Crabby Cradle; with this position, you can reach your G-spot well," I say to Emma.

"The second one is called Split Butterfly; it's a good position for clitoral stimulation."

"But was it worth it, such a risk?", I asked Emma.

Diamantha to readers: "Will be continued!"

Story 13

After a long divorce, we agreed on custody of the children. One week, the children were with me. The other week, the children were with their father.

This week is "Me-Time" week. It was a nice week for me.

I sat on the couch, bored. Most people I know are still married and busy with their families.

What am I going to do? I thought.

A friend of mine had advised me to start dating again.

To date?

To be honest, I wasn't looking forward to that. But I do miss sex now and then.

After thinking about it a lot, I decided to download a dating app. I find that easier because you have more choices.

I just put normal, boring pictures on the profile for fun.

Furthermore, I didn't put any pictures of the kids. I believe that, as a parent, you should protect your children. And it's no one's business what they look like.

There I am. On the couch, looking at profiles.

I get to see a lot of profiles that are far away.

Hey, finally someone who isn't that far along. I have a match with Hugo.

"Hi, cutie," he wrote.

"You have a nice appearance. I would like to get to know you. Would you like to come over for coffee at my house sometime?", he wrote.

What should I think now? He does look nice.

I feel my pussy starting to get wet at the thought of being fucked by Hugo after coffee.

Should I say yes? I hesitated.

I get up and walk to the kitchen. I grab a wine glass and fill it with the wine that was already on the counter.
Not only that, but I walk back to the couch with a glass of wine in my hand.
I take a sip. I put the glass of wine on the side table and picked up my phone again. I plop down on the couch again.

There I stood. In front of Hugo's door. Yes, I said yes. Should I ring the bell or not?
They say you live once, so I pressed the button.
There he stood, Hugo. Exactly like on his profile.
"Hi, come in," he said.
I walk inside. He closes the door behind me.
"I thought you might like to do something different. I didn't tell you everything," he said.
Suddenly, a man walks towards me.
What the hell is that? I thought.
"This is my partner, Samuel."
Wait, what? I thought.
"Hi, nice."
"Hi, Olivia, nice," I said in surprise.
"We are a bisexual couple," he continues.
What am I doing here? Should I leave now? I thought.
I continue to the living room.
"We enjoy having you here," says Hugo.
"You could have been open and honest with me," I said.
"A lot of people are a bit shocked by us. I've been honest with a woman before. At first, she was okay with it, but in the end, she didn't show up."
"Do you want something to drink?" said Samuel.
"Do you have any like Whiskey?"
"Certainly! I will arrange that for you," said Samuel.

I wasn't dressing sexy at all. I thought we'd have a drink, and then I'd drive home. Not only that, but I'm not okay with sex on a first date.

But what am I going to do in this situation? I'm already inside. I can run away too. But no, I stayed on the couch.

Samuel returns with a bottle of Whiskey and three Whiskey glasses.

He gave us both a glass and went to pour the Whiskey.

"Cheers to a nice evening," said Hugo.

"Cheers."

All three of us sat down on the couch.

It was quiet for a moment.

Hugo puts his hand on my left leg. Samuel puts his hand on my right leg.

They looked at me. At first, I felt trapped.

Should I leave now, or should I stay? I hesitated.

I haven't done anything exciting in a while.

I put my hand on Hugo's cheek. I looked deep into his eyes. I kiss him. Then I turn to Samuel. I hold his face and kiss him.

I take another sip of the Whiskey and stand up.

"Where is the bedroom?" I asked.

I take another sip of the Whiskey.

Hugo and Samuel looked at each other in surprise.

"So, you're looking forward to it," said Samuel.

"You don't have to do anything if you don't want to," Hugo said.

They stand up. "Walk with me," said Hugo.

I follow Hugo.

"This is the bedroom."

It is a large bedroom painted in light pink. In the middle is a large bed.

I fell onto the bed.

"Wow, it feels so nice and soft," I said.

Hugo and Samuel sat down next to me. They started caressing.
That felt great. Four hands are better than two, haha.
Hugo caressed my breasts while Samuel disappeared his hands
into my skirt.
"Ooo, you're so nice and wet," said Samuel.
He puts his hand in my pants and reaches my clitoris. He rubs my
clitoris with his finger. Then he puts two fingers in my vagina.
Hugo kisses me.
"I also want to feel how wet you are," Hugo said.
He puts two fingers in my vagina.
"Wow, four fingers in my vagina."
They moved their fingers together.
"I'm coming," I said.
They started moving their fingers faster.
I came hard.
"You can squirt so well," says Samuel.
"Mmmm...," Hugo moaned.
He licks my vagina clean.
"I want too," said Samuel.
Hugo moves aside and lets Samuel lick my pussy.
Hugo comes up and kisses me. I could taste myself, too.
Hugo opens my blouse and takes it off. He kisses my bare
breasts.
He quickly takes off his pants. I see a very large penis coming
out.
"Wow, what a big one you have," I said to Hugo.
He sucks on my nipples. He stands up and pushes his hard cock
into my mouth while Samuel licks my wet vagina.
"You're only getting wetter," says Samuel.
He stands up and quickly takes off his pants.
Before I knew it, he had put his penis in my vagina.
"You're so nice and wet. This feels so good," said Samuel.

Samuel goes in and out of my vagina hard with his penis.
I suck hard on Hugo's penis.
All three of us groan.
Who would have thought that all three of us would like this?
Samuel takes his penis out of my vagina.
"Get up," he said.
I went to get up. He lies on the bed.
"Come face me, so I can lick your pussy," he said.
"69, you mean?" I asked him.
"Yes, I want you to give me a nice blowjob," he said.
I lay down as he asked.
Hugo stood behind me and pushed his big cock deep into my ass.
"Ow, wow!" I shouted.
"Take it easy, Hugo," said Samuel.
"Are you okay?" he asked.
"Yes, you scared me. But I'm okay now."
He starts to move back and forth gently while Samuel licks my pussy.
He takes his penis out of my ass and lets Samuel suck his penis.
"Mmmm, your ass tastes delicious, Olivia," said Samuel.
Hugo puts his penis in my vagina and starts fucking my vagina hard.
"Oooo, ooo, oo," said Hugo.
"I'm coming," I said.
"Me too," said Hugo.
Hugo came inside me. He takes his penis out of me. Samuel and Hugo switched.
Hugo lay down on the bed and licked his cum clean.
Samuel stood behind me and went deep into my vagina with his penis.
Samuel starts thrusting hard into me while I'm sucking Hugo.
Not long later, Samuel came into my vagina.

"Oh, what a nice pussy you have, babe," said Samuel.
He lets his penis out of my vagina.

Hugo and I started licking his penis clean.

"What a horny experience," I said.
"Yes, but now I have a problem," Olivia said to me.

*Diamantha to readers:" What do you think the problem is?
Wait for part 2."*

Story 14

I was on my way to my parents. I have been living on my own for
two years now. I have a small studio in a student apartment
building. Very nice, of course. Something happens every day.
I always enjoy going to my parent's house every weekend. It's
two hours on the train. I've been sitting for an hour, so there's
still an hour to go.
With the internet, it will never be a boring ride.

The train stops, and a few people get off. People are coming in
again. A girl sits in front of me. She has short black hair with
black lipstick. She was dressed completely in black.
"Hello," she said.
"Hi"
"Have you been on the train for a while?" she asked.
"Yes, I have to sit for another hour. It's quite long, but I'm having
fun."
She smiles and says nothing more. She takes her phone out of
her jacket and goes on her phone.
I also continued watching my series.
Suddenly, she looked at me.
"I'm Linda, by the way," she said.
"Tiffanny."
We stare at each other without saying anything.
She gets up and grabs her bag.
"There's no station here. Are you getting out yet?" I asked.
"No, I'm going to the toilet," she says softly, giving me a wink.
After 1 minute, I get up and go to the toilet.
I knock on the door. Linda opens the door. She quickly pulls me
inside and quickly locks the door again.
I find this exciting. I never do crazy things like that. And not at all

with a stranger.

She presses me against the door while kissing me. I feel my pussy slowly getting wet.

What do I feel? How can I be wet? How can I find this hot? I like men, right? Maybe I'm wet from curiosity?

Mmmm... she's such a good kisser, I thought.

We undress.

She lowers the toilet seat and sits on it.

I sit on her lap, and we continue kissing.

Our breasts against each other.

Mmm, that's such a good feeling.

We stopped kissing. She grabs my breasts, and I grab her breasts. We massage each other's breasts.

"Get up," she says.

She grabs my hips with her hands and pushes my pussy against her face. She presses her nose against my clitoral area.

"What the fuck?" I said.

How strange is this? I thought.

But tasty.

Then I feel her tongue slide along my clitoral area along my thigh.

Mmmm, this is so delicious.

She puts two fingers in my vagina while sucking on my clitoral area.

I moan with pleasure.

She stops and stands up.

"Why did you stop? I haven't come yet," I said.

"That will come. Now it's my turn."

She pushes me down. She grabs my head with her two hands and pushes my head against her pussy.

"Lick it. Lick my wet pussy," she says.

I started licking her.

"Mmmmm, ... you have a nice tongue."
"Faster."
I move my tongue up and down faster.
She cums. I lick her pussy clean.
"Stand up," she says.
I get up. She takes a long black bondage rope from her bag.
"Turn around."
I turned around and looked in the mirror.
"Look in the mirror as I tie you up," she says.
"Do you know what the Egyptian mummy position is?" she
asked.
"No."
"Cross your wrists over your breasts."
"Oh, that's what you mean. Like the mummy."
"Yes, exactly."
I did my hands like the mummy. It looked pretty hot. Being tied
up naked on a train by a stranger.
I think she's an artist. She tied me up. The front looked like a
spider web.
She proudly took a picture of it.

"Can you show me the photo?" I asked Tiffanny.
"No".
"No? What happened then?" I asked.

She put on her clothes. She kissed me. She runs her tongue
down my belly button. She stops at my clitoral area. She sucks it
and pushes three fingers into me. She moves faster and faster.
Mmmmm, I moaned.
She went faster and faster until I came.
The train stops.
She quickly grabs her bag. She opens the door and closes it

quickly.

"Hey, hey, let me go!" I shouted.

She left me like this. Naked and tied up. She didn't say anything else.

"Have you reported it to the police?" I asked Tifanny.

Diamantha to readers: "Are you also curious? Wait for part 2."

Story 15

My girlfriend and I were looking at a site where you can meet single men. When we were on holiday in France, we downloaded the app out of curiosity. We wanted to see what kind of men were on the site. It is a special website only for elite people. It is also checked whether the details in your profile are correct. You must have a good, affordable job. You can think of managers, CEOs, and celebrities. My girlfriend has a good job, so she was able to register. On holiday, we met a couple when we were talking, and they said they had to leave because they had met someone through this app. That also made us curious. You are taking a risk because you pay ten thousand dollars when you register, but if your registration is rejected, you will not get your money back. I think that's theft, but those are the rules. You were also warned about it from the start.
Fortunately, my girlfriend's application was approved. Lucy doesn't find photos with profiles of Dick Picks interesting. Fortunately, you don't have that in this app. Everyone there is polite and respectful to each other. Fortunately, you can adjust to the environment. When we came home, we left the area and country the same as when we were on holiday. So France. Lucy had fallen in love with the French people. She thinks we can fly to France again for an adventure.

We came across a French businessman on the app.
"Hey, how are you? You have a nice photo on your profile," he writes.
Lucy walks to me and shows me the message.
"Shall I write to him back?" she asked.
"Do you like him?" I asked.
"He's a businessman. He is so successful, and he looks hot. He

looks neat," she says.

"Okay, you can write him back," I said.

"Hi, how are you? I'm here with my boyfriend on the app," she writes back.

"Oh, but it doesn't say on your profile that you are a couple. But that doesn't matter. It's more fun. I do indicate that I am straight," he writes back.

"That's not a problem for us. We are also a straight couple, but a horny one," she writes.

"Hahaha, nice and cozy," he writes.

"You also live in France, I assume!"

"No, we live in Florida," Lucy wrote.

"Oh, Florida, what a nice place."

"We were on holiday in France. I fell in love with the country and the people. Ooo, the food was so delicious. We will want to go there again."

"I have a business meeting in Florida next week. Would you like to meet?"

"Hey Michael, Daniel is in Florida next week for a business meeting," Lucy shouted.

"He'd like to meet us. What do you think?" she asked me.

"That seems like a good idea. We can show him enjoyable places here," I said to Lucy.

As agreed, we met with Daniel in a lunchroom.

"What time did you say?" I asked.

"One o'clock."

"Do you know there is a time difference between France and here?" I said, laughing.

"There he is," says Lucy.

Lucy walks towards him.

"Hey, how are you?" Lucy said.

"Good. I had to look for a while. My phone doesn't work very well. It's time for a new phone," he said, laughing.
"It's nice to have you here," said Lucy.
They walked together to the table where I was sitting.
"Hey, you must be Michael," he said.
"Yes, please sit down," I said.
"I have to tell you right away that I don't have much time. I have to leave in fifteen minutes," says Daniel.
"Oo, that's a shame," said Lucy.
"Yes, it took so long to find the location. I didn't want to cancel the appointment, so I came anyway, even if it was for fifteen minutes. Then I have another meeting. I'm always so busy," he continues.
"What do you want to drink?" I said.
"Coca-Cola," said Lucy.
"Me too," Michael said.
"I'm going to place the order at the bar. That's always faster," I said.
I got up and walked to the bar. I come back with three Coca-Cola in my hand.
"Here you are," I said, and I put the glasses on the table.
"I'm in Florida every three weeks. We're developing a project," Daniel said.
"Have you met more often via the app?" Lucy asked.
"No, you're the first. As you know, I'm busy. I was on the train, and I happened to open the app and came across your message."
"I'm thinking about buying an apartment here. Do you have a nice suggestion?" he said.
"There are impressive apartments in our area. It's a bit expensive, but you have a nice view, and it's also quiet," said Lucy.

"If you need help styling your home, I can help you with it," I said.

"I can email you with what's for sale in our area," said Lucy.

"Yes, please," he said.

We drink the coke.

"Guys, I have to go now. I can't be late. Nice to meet you guys. Shall I pay the bill?" Daniel said.

"No, don't worry. We'll stay for dinner," Lucy said.

"We still speak on the phone," he said.

"Yes, we still keep in touch," Lucy said.

We say goodbye to him, and he walks away.

In the meantime, Lucy has emailed him a few sales options. He had seen a nice apartment, and he wanted to view it with us.

Lucy knows the real estate agent, and he trusts her with the key to the apartment. He hopes that Lucy will sell the apartment for him.

When Daniel was in town, we agreed with him that we would wait for him at the apartment.

Lucy and I walk around the apartment to make sure everything is neat and clean.

We heard the bell ring.

"Shall I open it?" I asked.

"Yes".

I walked to the door, and there he was standing in front of the door with a bottle of wine.

"I brought this from France, especially for you," said Daniel.

"That's very nice. Thank you," I said, taking the wine.

"Come on in."

"Hey, nice to see you again," Lucy said, kissing him on the cheek.

"He brought us a French wine," I said, showing it to Lucy.

"Oh, how sweet of you," Lucy said.

"So... This is the apartment you were talking about," he said.

"Yes, let me show you. The real estate agent is a friend of mine. He gave me the key, and he told me everything about the apartment," said Lucy.

"Ha… So he's not coming himself?" Daniel asked.

"No, I'm the real estate agent today," Lucy said.

We walk around the apartment and show Daniel the apartment.

"In addition to a nice big kitchen, we have a large bedroom with a queen-sized bed," Lucy said, and we walked into the bedroom.

Lucy sits on the edge of the bed.

"It feels good. Are you coming to test the bed too?" she asked me and Daniel.

Daniel sat on her left, and I sat on her right.

Lucy turns to Daniel and kisses him on the mouth.

I was in complete shock. We had not discussed this.

She turns around and kisses me on the mouth too.

She puts her left hand on Daniel's leg and her right hand on my leg. "How do you like the queen-size bed?", she asked.

"It feels good," Daniel said.

Lucy looks at Daniel and gives him a French kiss.

I was in complete shock. I still didn't know what I saw.

What should I say? I thought.

What should I think about this?

Lucy looks at me and gives me a French kiss.

"What do you think, honey?" she asked.

"I e… I…," I stuttered.

"Do you like it too?" she asked, looking deep into my eyes.

"Yes, nice," I said shyly.

Lucy falls back onto the bed.

Daniel starts caressing her breasts. I looked at them.

What should I do? I thought.

I put my hand on her legs and started caressing her. She is spoiled on both sides—double pleasure.

She gets up, takes off her dress and bra, and goes back into bed.
Daniel and I were going to do the same.
There we were, all three sitting next to each other on the bed.
We have changed places. I started caressing her breasts, and
Daniel started playing with her clitoris.
"What a nice woman you have. She tastes good," Daniel said.
"Did you hear that? I'm lucky to have you," I said, giving her a
French kiss.
I looked up.
Daniel grabs her feet and starts fucking her in a missionary
position. At that moment, I felt my penis getting harder. I started
pulling him until he got nice and hard. I stood behind Daniel.
"Shall I join you?" I asked.
Daniel squatted forward with Lucy's legs in his hand and his
penis in her vagina.
This way I can reach it better, I thought, and I put my penis in her
ass.
"Oooo." Lucy moaned as she rubbed her clitoris.

*"You see your girlfriend fucking someone else, and all you feel
is love for her?" I asked Michael.*
"Yes, we don't have jealousy," says Michael.
*"Nice Missionary Double, but can you understand that not
everyone can?" I asked.*
Then it was quiet. Michael was thinking.

To be continued in Part 2!

Story 16

We had booked a hotel in New York. We had to save for a long time to make this dream come true. What is my dream? You'll find out soon.

I had to convince my husband and believe me, it wasn't easy. Who would agree to something like that? It would affect his norms and values.

One day, he came home after work.

"We're going to pack. We're going to New York for a weekend. Bring sexy clothes and nice lingerie," he said.

"Vincent, what are we going to do there?" I asked.

"That's a surprise," he says, laughing.

He checks his phone very often. He's behaving very strangely. What is he up to, I thought.

"Put on your sexy clothes. We'll go to the hotel first. We'll put down our suitcases and go straight to a café nearby," he said.

We put our suitcases in the room and went straight to the café. It was very enjoyable in the café. People were sitting at the bar, having drinks, and chatting. There were also people dancing with their drinks in their hands.

He's constantly checking his phone and looking around.

"You've been constantly on your phone the last few days. I'm not used to that. What's going on?" I asked him.

He keeps looking around without saying anything.

"Are you looking for someone? Who are you looking for?" I asked him.

"Ah, there he is," he said. He grabs my hand and walks to a tall, dark man.

Mmmm... Who is that sexy? I thought.

"Eva, Emiliano. Emiliano, Eva," he said.

We shake hands.

"This is the person who will make your dream come true," he said.

"My dream?" I asked surprised.

"Shall we go for a drink?" asked Emiliano.

"Just give me Bacardi Cola," Vincent said.

"For me too," I said.

"Three Bacardi Colas," Emiliano said to the bartender.

I thought you weren't going to tell me he's a Gigolo.

No, that is not possible. He looks like a businessman.

"Vincent told me you two have been married for years?" he said.

"Yes, we are happily married," I said.

"She kept insisting that she wanted to try some other things outside our relationship," Vincent said.

"I had to think about it for a long time. I mean, you don't want to lose each other."

He looks at me and kisses me in the mouth.

"I see that the love is still there," says Emiliano.

The three of us went dancing.

Vincent looks at his phone.

"Hey, it's going to rain heavily soon," says Vincent.

The three of us walk to the hotel.

"Vincent said you've been under a lot of stress the last few days. I can help you with it," Emiliano says.

"Take off your clothes and lie on your stomach."

I take off my clothes and lie on the bed in my lingerie.

Vincent takes scented candles from his suitcase and lights them.

Emiliano takes off his clothes, leaving only his boxer shorts on.

Vincent takes massage oil from his suitcase.

"Today you will be completely spoiled, darling," says Vincent.

He gives the massage oil to Emiliano.

Vincent dims the lights and takes a seat on a chair.

Emiliano drops a few drops on my back.

"I'm going to start at your shoulders. If I squeeze too hard, you have to say so," Emiliano says.

"That's okay," I said, closing my eyes.

I feel his muscular hands squeezing my tight shoulders. He squeezed the muscles of my upper back and also the tissue of the muscles of my lower back.

He presses against my muscles with the thumbs of each hand. He moves his thumbs in small circles.

"Mmmm…," I moaned.

He kneads the muscles in my neck with his thumbs. He squeezes the muscles that run down to the spine with the heels of his hand. He moves along the back of my neck in circular movements.

He puts some oil in his hand. He goes down again with his hands. Now it's my thighs' turn.

I wet my lips. I bite my lip.

"You can move your hand more to the center," I said hornily.

He moves his hands more to the center, to my string. He takes off my thong and starts massaging my vagina.

"Mmmmm…," I moaned.

"What a nice, horny woman you are," Emiliano whispered in my ear.

"Are you enjoying yourself, baby?",Vincent asked as he looked at us.

"Huhmm," I groaned.

"Turn around," Emiliano said.

He puts oil in his hand again and starts massaging my feet. He runs his hands down my legs to my vagina. He puts his thumbs on my clitoris and makes small circles.

He carefully inserts a finger into my vagina. He then adds two more fingers and starts making a circular motion with his fingers. I've never experienced this before.

I feel an orgasm coming quickly, and I start to shake.

"Are you coming, baby?" added Vincent while he played with himself.

"I'm coming, babe," I said.

"Come for me, baby," Vincent said.

Emiliano moves his fingers faster and faster.

I came.

Emiliano gives me a passionate kiss.

"You did well," Emiliano said.

He gets up, takes off his boxer shorts, and holds his penis.

"Are you ready for this?" he asked as he started moving his penis back and forth.

He sits in front of me and grabs my legs. He puts my left leg on his left shoulder and my right leg on his right shoulder. My legs hang over his shoulder.

He goes inside me. He goes in and out of my vagina hard with his penis.

He lifts my pelvis so he can fill every inch with my vagina.

I have the best husband in the world, I thought.

This is the best surprise of my life, I thought as he thrust his penis into me.

"Is it good, babe? Getting fucked by another cock?" Vincent asked in a horny voice.

"Uhm...," I groaned.

"I'm coming again, baby," I said.

"Come on, beautiful woman," Emiliano said.

I came for the second time.

He takes his penis out of my vagina.

"Stand up."

I stood up, and he lay on his back.

"Come lay with your back on me," he said.

I lay on top of him and put my face against his face. He puts his penis in my vagina and spreads my legs. He holds my legs with his hands. He raises his legs and starts thrusting from his hips.

"Play with yourself," he whispered in my ear.

I won't let myself be told that twice.

Vincent stood in front of us so he could see better. He watched Emiliano moved his penis in and out of my vagina.

"Enjoy babe. Oh, you are so soaking wet, darling," he said while he masturbated.

"I'm coming," I moaned.

I came for the third time.

"I'm going to come deep inside you. Get up and lie on your back," Emiliano said.

I stood up, and so did he. I lay down in his place.

"Put your legs up high and hold your pelvis high with your hands.

"I'll try," I said.

"Come on, I'm going to help you," Vincent said,

He stood in front of my head and held my legs high so that my hips stayed high. Emiliano bends over with his back to me and inserts his penis deep into my vagina.

He started thrusting hard while Vincent held my legs. After a few thrusts, Emiliano came deep inside me.

"Oh, that was so good," said Emiliano. He gets off the bed and walks to the bathroom.

Vincent dropped my legs onto the bed.

"Come, I'll let you come too," I told Vincent.

I put his penis in my mouth and started sucking hard.

"Ooo, you're a horny, naughty woman. Ooo...you do that so well," Vincent moaned.

He takes his penis out of my mouth and squirts all over my face. He gives me a French kiss and licks my face clean.

"Thanks for the surprise," I said to him and kissed him.
"You're welcome. I'll pay for it with your credit card," he says, laughing.

"Mmm… wonderful Folded Guard. That's the name of the first position," I say to Eva.
"Nice and stretched wide open, that's what the Split Sinner position is like," I say.
"Squatting Pile Driver 180 is the third position. You can also try it with anal penetration."

"Hahaha, he dares," says Eva.
"What do you mean?" I asked.

Part 2 is to be continued!

Story 17

During the day, I am a sports masseur. But in the evening, I give tantra massage.

A client of mine was curious about tantra. During the day, she came to me for a sports massage, and in the evening, she would come to me for a tantra massage.

"Put on nice, flexible clothes. I'll see you tonight," I said to Eugene.

It's seven o'clock. The bell is ringing. She is always on time. I open the door.

"Hey, Eugene, come in."

She comes in and takes off her coat.

"Sit down. Would you like a cup of tea or coffee?"

"Go ahead, tea," she said.

"Let's have something warm to drink to warm ourselves up." We took a few sips of the tea.

"I always start with meditation first so that we can free our minds for tantra."

I have already placed large mats on the floor in the room. But first, we will meditate on the chair.

"Come sit opposite me. Place your feet directly under your knees. The feet should point straight forward. Make sure that your back, head, and neck are in line. Do not put your back against the back of the chair. This ensures that you're not going to fall asleep. Put your hands on your legs. Close your eyes," I said.

"You have to open yourself up to a next-level experience and connection," I said.

"What is tantra for you, and what do you hope its purpose is?"

"Are you mentally prepared for this?"

"Be in the here and now."

After five minutes of meditation, we started.

I made everything comfortable. I have prepared soft pillows and candles.

"We're going to start soon. We're going to make sure you are self-aware. Everything you feel is welcome. Don't hide your feelings."

We sat down on the measurements I placed on the floor.

We sat cross-legged, facing each other, with our knees touching each other.

I looked at her, deep into her eyes, as I touched her tenderly.

"Do you feel my touch?", I asked Eugene.

"Yes."

"We're going to focus on breathing," I said.

"You breathe from your abdomen and let it out through the nose."

"Breathe."

Eugene looks at her belly.

"Exhale."

"Keep looking at me. We have to keep eye contact."

"It's not easy," Eugene said.

"Open your mouth a little. Not all the way open. Open a little bit. We're going to do it together."

We started breathing together from the abdomen and exhaling from the nose while looking at each other.

"I'm going to touch you now, but it is not allowed to have an orgasm. When you feel an orgasm, you have to focus on your breathing. By focusing on your breathing, you regain control over your body."

"Are you ready?" I asked Eugene.

I move my fingertips over her body. Touching her like that wakes up her nerves. After a while, I moved on to the next level.

"Take off your clothes. You can keep your bra and pants on. Lie on your stomach," I said.

I got up and grabbed a heated massage oil. I opened the back of her bra and let it fall. I put a little massage oil on her back. I ran my hands over her back.

"Are you feeling relaxed?" I asked.

"Yes, it's wonderful."

I massage her buttocks slowly and intensely, and I squeeze her buttocks. I know this can be very exciting for some people.

I heard her moan.

"Keep focusing on your breathing. Stay relaxed."

I take off my clothes and cover myself completely with the massage oil.

"Stay relaxed and be surprised."

I lay down on her quietly. I slide my breasts against her buttocks. I hear her moaning again.

"Continue to focus on your breathing," I repeated.

I put my hands under her stomach while I continued to slide against her buttocks with my lower body.

I sit next to her again.

"You can take off the rest of your clothes and lie on your back."

She takes off her bra and pants and lies on her back. I put massage oil on her stomach. I slide my hands from her stomach to her breasts. I massaged her breasts. I take her nipples between my thumbs and index fingers. I run my hands to her legs and between her legs. I notice she's starting to get a little wet.

"Concentrate on breathing. Breathe in from your abdomen; breathe out from your nose," I told her while I massaged her clitoris.

"I'm almost here," she said.

"I think it's a good time to end this session. We'll continue next week," I told her.

I grab a clean towel and wipe away the oil.

"I think Tantra is a beautiful way to connect with others. You have to embrace your feelings. Is it desire, anger, or rage? It doesn't matter."
"Tantra is not about orgasm but about sexual energy. Every time you build up sexual energy. This allows you to wake up your nervous system, and you can feel more. And in the end, the orgasm is more intense."
"I did indeed experience that. But we didn't just stop there," Meghan said.
"What do you mean?" I asked Meghan.

To be continued!

Story 18

It is a sultry evening.

"Come in, come in," he said as he held the door open for me. I chuckled at his enthusiasm and got into the car. I like gallant men. Fortunately, Christian is one of them.

"Hello, beautiful," says Christian.

"Hello, handsome," I said, and I kissed him on the cheek. He turns on the car, and we drive away.

"We agreed on three," he said.

He puts his hand under my dress.

"Mmm… I don't feel any pants."

He puts his hand on my breasts.

"I don't feel a bra."

"No, I used a special adhesive tape."

"We agreed that you would only wear three pieces of clothing. I only count one, and that is the dress."

"You forgot the shoes."

"That's two; which one is number three?"

"Number three is a surprise."

"A surprise? What is it? Do you still have to wear it?" he asked.

After a few minutes of driving, we arrived at our destination. Christian had reserved a table at a nice restaurant by the sea. We took a seat at our table.

"Would you like something to drink?" he asked.

"Yes, just water."

"Water? You're so boring."

I always take water when I go out with a stranger. I feel safer with water.

"If that were the case, I wouldn't have agreed to meet you. And I wouldn't have gotten into your car either," I said, giving him a wink.

"What can I pour for you?" asked the waiter".

"Red wine and Coca-Cola, please," said Christian.

"It will be arranged for you," said the waiter, and he walked away.

"Coca-Cola? I said water."

"There's no difference, right? Coca-Cola is boring, too."

I felt the nerves running through my body.

Here I am. We agreed that neither of us wanted to be in a relationship. We wanted to discover new things and enjoy each other. Enjoy without obligations. Enjoy without expectations. Only sex. Only hot and wild sex. We both lacked sex. We help each other. The arrangement was that simple. Help each other. I look at him intensely. I see his lips moving, but I have no idea what he's saying. Would he be better than Anthony? I thought.

"Are you going to tell me what number three is?" he asked curiously.

"No, that's a surprise."

"Come here."

I got up and sat next to him. I heard my heart pounding and my breathing increasing.

"Come sit on my lap."

I sat on his lap. I felt his hands sliding on my buttocks. I look deep into his eyes. His eyes shine. I feel he wanted me. He gives me an intense kiss. I bite his lower lip. He presses my body against his.

"I have a surprise for you too. You have to trust me."

He takes something out of his pocket and immediately runs his hands under my dress. He inserts something cold into my vagina. I tried to stifle a groan. What is it? I have no idea, but it feels cold and hot at the same time.

"You can sit back in your seat." I stood up and sat across from him again.

We take the menu and look at what specialty they have.

"I'm in the mood for fish," I said.

"I'm craving meat—lots of meat," he said.

Before I could answer, I felt a tingling vibration in my vagina.

"Ooo...," I moaned.

"Not so loud; we're in a restaurant. Remember?" he said, laughing.

He takes the remote control out of his pocket and places it on the table. He presses a button. It started shaking harder.

"Oh, what the fuck is that?"

"They are vaginal balls that I bought especially for you." He presses a button again.

"Can you feel them vibrating? Wonderful?"

I gasped.

Oo...that's so hot. I pressed my thighs together. It felt more intense. I felt those balls hitting every inch of my vagina.

"Can you hold on? You're not allowed to cum."

"Take it off. I can't hold on anymore, no. Please take it off."

"Okay, I'm going to take it off," he says, looking deep into my eyes and taking a sip of the wine.

"I can't take it anymore. This is unbearable." My body shakes. I felt a hard orgasm coming. Then he took it off.

"I said, you can't cum right now."

He stood up. He takes money out of his wallet and throws it on the table.

"Let's go. I feel like fucking you."

We drove to a forest that is very crowded during the day, but at night it is terrifying to be there. We got out of the car.

"Can I take the balls out now?" I asked.

He picks me up and puts me on the hood. He roughly pulls up my dress.

"Let Me Do That."

His face disappeared between my legs.

I felt his hand slide into my vagina. He takes out the balls.

He quickly undoes his belt and flies. He takes his penis out of his pants.

"Fuck foreplay."

He puts his hard penis in my horny, wet vagina and starts thrusting hard.

He sucks and bites my nipple hard.

I moaned with pleasure. He puts his fingers in my mouth.

"Ssshhtt, don't shout. We'll be attacked soon."

I take his fingers in my mouth and suck them.

He pulled me off the car and turned me around.

"Oh..", he said.

"Surprise. That's number three."

He had discovered the butt plug.

"What a nice surprise," he whispered in my ear.

I want nothing more than to finally feel his cock inside me again.

"Spread your legs." He pushes me onto the hood. He slaps me on my butt. He pushes his penis into my vagina again and starts thrusting deeply.

"Wet my fingers," he says as he puts his hand in my mouth.

He removes his penis from my vagina and removes the butt plug from my ass. He wets my asshole with his wet fingers. He pulls my buttocks apart and pushes his penis deep into my ass. I cried out. He stood still for a moment without moving.

"Don't move; he needs some time to get used to it," he said.

He starts thrusting slowly. The pain has been replaced by pleasure. After a few thrusts, he takes his penis out and squirts all over my foot.

"Could he have replaced Anthony?" I asked Samira.

"There's more," Samira said.

"Ow! Tell me."

"It turns out he has a fetish," Samira continues.

"Fetish? No, wait. You're not telling me he…"

To be continued in Part 2.

Story 19

I didn't sleep very well, but I still have a night shift. That's quite tough for me. I get out of the car, sighing and tired.

I don't feel like doing this, I thought.

But yes, the invoices have to be paid. Put on a poker face and go, Carla, I thought.

I received the transfer from a colleague.

"I don't expect anything crazy. There is a new patient," she says.

"He's hot," she whispered in my ear.

"You'll see," she says, winking at me.

I'm tired and a little grumpy. No hot patient can make my night better, I thought.

"Well, I'm going. Good luck!" says my colleague. She packs her things and walks away.

I became curious and went straight to Room 90. It is a department only for elite people.

I open the door and see a hot man lying on the bed. He had an accident, and he had to stay in the hospital for a few days for a check-up.

"Good evening. I am your nurse for tonight. My name is Carla," I said to him.

In this department, patients have the luxury of staying alone in the room.

"Good evening, Nurse Carla; you will spoil me this evening," he said, winking at me.

What a hottie! I think he's ready to go home already, I thought.

"If you need anything, you can press the emergency button," I said.

"Stay on task, Carla," I told myself.

"I certainly will," he said.

I walk away and pass the other patients in the ward.

I notice that I am no longer tired and grumpy.

If I had a nice patient like Felix every day, I would come to work every day without complaining, I thought.

I find myself getting a little horny at the thought. How can I think I'm fucking a patient. No, no, no, that's not possible. It's forbidden, Carla. Sex with a patient? No, that is not possible. This is a hospital, not a brothel!

It's a naughty thought, but the idea still makes me horny and wet.

It's just the two of us today. Many colleagues have reported being sick.

It is two in the morning. An emergency button is pressed. My colleague went to see what was going on.

An emergency button is pressed again. I see it's coming from Felix's room. My heart starts beating hard.

I walk to his room and open the door.

"There's my favorite nurse. I hoped you would come," he said.

"Can I help you with anything?" I said.

"Yes, look!" he said, pointing to his penis, which had a hard erection.

"What's with it?" I asked him.

"Did you give me erection pills? Or is it you? I was thinking about you all the time. I have never seen a hot, sexy nurse before. I would be sick every day just to see you."

"Can I hold your hand?" he asked.

"Yes, that's allowed."

I feel my pussy getting wetter.

Behave, Carla. Get it out of your head. This is not possible!

"Can I move your hand?" he asked, holding my hand.

"If you don't want to, you have to say so."

"I can check and feel what is causing it. But first, I have to see and feel whether it is a real erection," I said.

He let go of my hand and I walked to the door. I lock the door. I walk back to the bed. I put my hands under the blanket. I hold his penis with my hands.
"I can confirm that it is a real one," I said.
"You can also feel whether it is a real erection," he said.
I climb onto the bed with my back to him.
I put his rock-hard penis inside me.
"Oh, that feels like a real erection," I said hornily.
"Mmmm…," he moaned.
I stretch my legs forward and slowly start to rotate my hips.
"What a nice, horny nurse you are," he moaned.
"Sshhhtt…. Not so loud," I told him.
After a few thrusts, we came.

"What a delightful quickie with Lazy Rodeo! That's the name of the position. The tension makes it extra hot," I said.

"I needed it. My husband hasn't touched me in a long time," Carla says.

"Were you caught? Or did other patients hear you?" I asked Carla.

Diamantha to readers: "Are you also curious? Wait for Part 2! "

Story 20

She uses a long rope. She ties my wrists together behind my back. She wraps the rest of the rope, my arms to my body. She puts the rope between my arms and torso and squeezes it tightly.

She then slaps me hard in the face.

"Are you going to obey today?"

"Yes, Mistress Lily," I said.

"Who? I can't hear you."

She's going to hit me again.

"Yes, Mistress Lily," I said louder.

During the day, I am the director of a well-known telecom company. I manage more than 400 employees. But when I close the door, I am not a director. Then I am submissive. I like not being in charge for a while. I like to obey. To be abused.

She takes a black tickler and starts tickling me under my armpits.

"You know what the rules of the game are."

"Yes, Mistress."

I started laughing. She slaps me in the face.

"I said... You know what the rules are," she says.

"Yes, Mistress."

She puts the tickler under my balls and starts tickling.

I couldn't contain my laughter and started laughing again. She slaps me in the face.

"You disobedient slave. I will teach you a lesson."

She walks to the kitchen and returns with a mandarin in her hand.

"Open your mouth."

I opened my mouth, and she popped the mandarin into my mouth.

She takes the tickler again and tickles my balls and my penis.

It's hard for me to laugh with a mandarin in my mouth.

I started laughing again. She squeezes my balls.

"What do you understand about the word… obey?" she said.

She moves the tickler toward my breasts. I spit the mandarin out of my mouth and started laughing hard.

She puts the Tickler down. She takes a red "Hot Wax Candle" and lights it.

"Do you want more? Do you want to obey now?"

"Yes, mistress."

She drops wax from the candle on my breasts.

"Mm mm…," I moaned.

She knows how to slap me in the face.

"Did I give you permission to moan?"

She slaps me again.

"No Mistress. Sorry Mistress."

"Mistress … "Who?" she asked as she grabbed my face hard.

"Mistress Lily," I said.

She slaps me in the face again.

"Well done."

She drops wax from the candle on my back.

I held back my moan. How difficult that is! Nice and submissive.

"You have an important public job. I know that no one should know what you do secretly," I said to Charles.

"How did you meet your Mistress?", I asked Charles.

Part 2 for more!

Are you going on an adventure?

Please protect yourself. Use a condom!

Thank You

My thanks go to Team Goozlyzo. Thank you for believing in me. I would not have had the courage to publish the book without you.

My thanks go out to YOU! Thank you for buying the book. I hope you've trained your imagination. I hope this helped you come.

Read it several times, and don't forget to share it with everyone you know.

Do you want to stay informed about upcoming books?

Follow us on :
www.instagram.com/diamanthapearl
www.goozlyzo.com
www.diamanthapearl.com

We're not ready. This is just the beginning!

Nice to meet you!

Upcoming

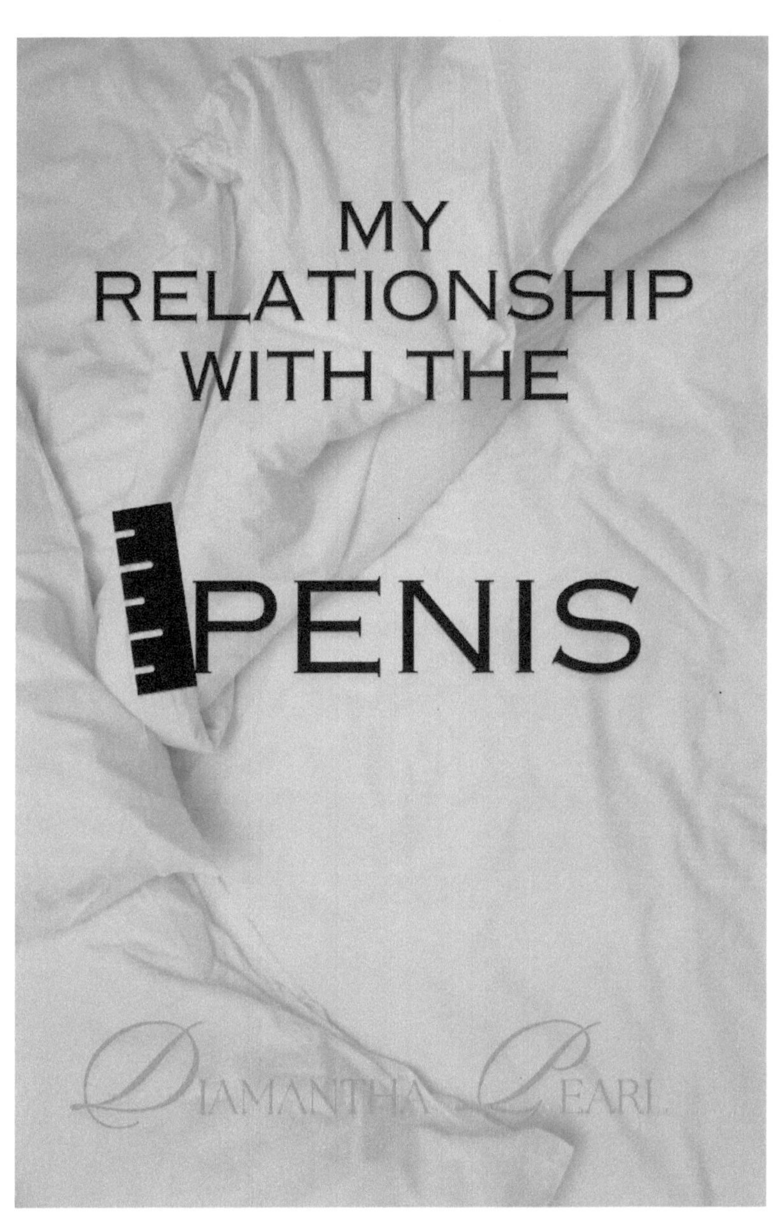

Upcoming

www.ingramcontent.com/pod-product-compliance
Lightning Source LLC
LaVergne TN
LVHW091725190726
843493LV00001B/454